Chapter One

'Silently falls the rain, gently and drippingly on my sodden, soddening hair.'

"Oops, it's lucky David isn't here to read the barbarous use I've just made of the Queen's English," said a half-drenched figure to himself, bringing forth a warm smile on this miserable night.

Both his self-reproach and his wistful grin were produced by the fond memory of his English teacher at secondary school and provoked by what he had just written on a postcard bought on the spur of a sentimental moment.

"What sarcastic comment would you have condemned me with, sir?" he asked himself.

Already imagining the possible answers, he shrugged his shoulders to the rules of grammar, turned his collar to the evening drizzle and continued to write while making a heroic attempt at keeping the card dry and therefore 'sendable':

'In spite (or because) of the weather, I couldn't resist the writing of this little seaside message of hope. Just remember: The world always sparkles AFTER THE RAIN!

Wish you were here.

He smiled again with childish excess at his self-acclaimed, albeit peculiar literary originality while slipping the slightly soggy piece of old-fashioned tourist merchandising into the pocket of his jacket. "Hey, that's the second in just a few minutes," he told himself, referring to the grin that he now happened to be showing to the dark-suited stranger who had suddenly appeared at his side; lately (to put it mildly, as is the British custom) his face had lost the smile that had hitherto resided there since as far back as he could remember. In fact, one shopkeeper he regularly visited as a younger man had once asked him why on earth he was grinning every time he came through the establishment door. 'The smiler', as he had been dubbed thereafter, never could give an answer that met with the standards of logic. It was simply one of the traits - or treats – that he had always offered up to the world.

- "Good evening, sir. Any problem? Can I be of assistance?" asked the newcomer from under the moisture filled aura of the awful yellow light that shone above his head.

The man who had been sitting, thinking, writing, smiling and talking by himself in the roguish twilight looked closer at the uniformed stranger who had so politely shown concern for his well-being, starting with the heavy black shoes and on upwards to the wet face looking seriously down at him; or perhaps it was a serious face looking wetly down at him? He certainly was in the strangest of moods today, he thought to himself, as yet restraining himself from entering into conversation.

At once he noticed that beside the officer stood another darkly, but this time plain-clothes suited figure. His companion wasn't a policeman, however; she was a female detective who appeared in the gloom to be some twenty-five years younger than her male counterpart, which made her to be around the same age as himself -if his calculations weren't outrageously off the mark. She was also found rather attractive by the nostalgic writer of postcards. He, on the other hand, received an enigmatic and, it seemed to him, not altogether friendly look from her.

Not that it surprised him in the slightest. There was no need for a great deal of imagination to see that, from the uniformed team's point of view, he must have looked anything but elegant, sitting as he was on the curb of the pavement with both feet stretched out into the roadside - and on an evening that was meant to be enjoyed looking out from the inside of a welcoming dwelling. He felt sure that the only prop missing was the bottle of cheap spirits in the inside pocket of the raincoat that covered his tattered suit.

- "Good evening to you, officer," he finally said to the elder of the two, "I was on my way to my hotel –look, it's right there on the next corner– after having taken a long, long yearned-for stroll when I decided that it was time to rest my weary legs and –of equal importance- make good use of it."

- "Good use of it did you say? Of what exactly, if you don't mind the asking?"

- "Time, my honorable keeper of the law. Although it must be said that it is to be seen if the use of the term 'good use of' is the most adequate. You know," he finished talking to himself once more, "I just bet there's another flaw somewhere in that last sentence."

All of a sudden, the policeman's round face lit up and he snapped his fingers enthusiastically. "Well of course! I haven't the foggiest idea of what you are talking about, but I do recognize your face. This morning it was; I'd just come on duty when I saw a crowd of people outside the art gallery not far from the station. I took a walk over and there you were in the doorway being photographed. Don't tell me, let me think. Mr..... Penrose, isn't it? You're a famous painter, I believe. On a day like this you'd have to use water-colours, wouldn't you?" he ended with a chuckle.

After his witticism (or so he liked to call it) was ungraciously ignored, the policeman cleared his throat and went back to his role as the serious law enforcement officer.

- "But what on earth are you doing sitting by the roadside in the rain?" he continued. "I know that you artistic people are a bit weird –no offence meant– but this is a bit far out, wouldn't you say?"

- "Ah, forgive me. I'm not ranting, as you probably think, or raving, as you seem to suppose. Let me explain," the drenched figure replied as he handed to the puzzled sergeant the evidence that he thought to be the proof of his words.

- "You see? I was simply sat sitting here -as someone somewhat comically said- writing a postcard, as one does –or at least used to do- when on a visit to a coastal town like the one in which you've probably made your happy home and which I'm on a visit to. Maybe you or your silently engaging colleague could indicate the whereabouts of a post-box so that it can be on its way post-haste and as quickly as possible. It's an old-fashioned surprise for someone back home."

The mature policeman's bewildered look didn't change, however. On the contrary, once he had ever so quickly, and even more discreetly, read over what was written, his face took on an expression of complete astonishment.

- "Yes, I certainly do see, Mr. Penrose. And I don't have the slightest doubt about the face that this someone is going to put on when the card arrives. You leave it with me and I'll make sure it gets safely on its way."

- "Oh really? Do you mean to say that you know the person in question?"

- "You could say that, in a manner of fashion. I'm good at my job," the police officer asserted enigmatically while stretching out a hand to help Mr. Penrose to his feet. Once up, the presumed artist looked sideways at his helper as all three now strolled towards the hotel.

- "Then you certainly are undervalued walking the beat," the newly arrived stranger graciously offered. "Your deductive prowess is wasted on aiding lost souls like me find post-boxes and escorting them to their hotels. In any case, why don't you call me Roger. You can tell me your name and that will make us intimate enough for me to let you in on three little secrets about myself. It may sound quite strange, but I haven't related to someone so quickly since I was an easy-going young lad. Just something else I´ve lost over the years," he finished under his breath.

- "Well in the first place, Jack," he went on, having been furnished with the name that the officer´s parents had lovingly given him, "in the first place, although my surname is Penrose, I´m not an artist at all, and therefore the term famous isn´t applicable either. To tell you the truth, I'm a totally uncreative type who works – correction; worked for- a very large, very private finance company, and who decided to take a day trip to the seaside town that he used to visit as a young whippersnapper every summer with his parents. So, there you have it; not too long ago I said my goodbyes and bid my farewells to my fellow workmates and after a few months of kind of wandering around, here I am. Oh, don´t worry," Roger continued with his unexpected outpour, "for although I celebrated no more than my thirty-ninth birthday a few weeks ago, my financial situation will allow me to live more than comfortably for the rest of my days and nights. You see, I was very good at making money, both for my employers as well as for the brilliant young man they so astutely employed. Anyway, and all that apart, you just happened to see me this morning having my photo taken alongside the aforementioned painter who just happens to share the same surname as myself. That´s why I went to take a closer look, in fact. I thought he might be a long-lost half-brother of mine. But that´s a story we won´t go into right now. So, your confusion is perfectly understandable; and does you no disservice. Don´t ask me how the photo bit happened; I was just kind of sucked into the situation without being invited to do so."

Jack and his so far nameless companion listened attentively, surprised that this stranger should be telling them his life-story; but not half as much as the storyteller, who carried on with his tale, just as he said he would.

- "But that's neither here nor there, is it. Let's get back to the present and to my second secret before I do start talking a lot of nonsensical gibberish - always supposing the word *secret* to be the correct term to use. Well, the fact is that the postcard is now heading it's happy way to the darling woman who quite literally brought me into this world; unaided and with no less than her own hands, would you believe?"

Jack took another look at the postcard, just to double check the address. Although wrong about the financier being a painter, he knew without a doubt the recipient of the postcard's *real* identity; Roger, the policeman perceived, was sincere in his affirmation, yet was plainly the victim of some kind of self-wrought confusion. He decided, nonetheless, to play along -just for the moment.

- "Couldn't she make it with you, then? I suppose that's why you seem to be a bit down in the dumps." he finished sympathetically. He too was beginning to feel a certain empathy with the bedraggled and miserable looking character walking alongside him.

- "Another good observation, Jack. And one that just happens to bring me to my third confession; I didn't tell her that I was coming. I wanted to re-live the memories on my own. Isn't that a terrible thing to have done? Shouldn't I have made it a family return? And doesn't it say a lot about my personal situation? Emotionally speaking, you understand."

He continued without waiting for an unwanted answer. "I felt that I had to come alone, that it wasn´t one of those trips down memory lane that you can share with someone. You know what I mean? When you can laugh at yourself and say *'oh look, this is the place where I shared my first ice cream with such and such a girl and who purposely buried my nose in her cone before running off giggling.'* And I'll add something more; I think I know the reason behind not wanting anyone with me. You see, I had the oddest sense of walking around all day looking for someone, and that this ´someone´ is the person I wanted to be with. In fact," he finished saying, thoughtfully fingering his soggy, stubbly chin, "If you think about it, that was probably the principal motive that pushed me to make the journey in the first place."

- "Perhaps you were looking for that mischievous playmate, or someone else you had struck up an important friendship with and who you´d like to meet up with again," put in Jack.

- "That would appear to be the obvious answer to the enigma. On the other hand, I get the feeling that it has to do with some unsuspected personality – or with someone I've completely forgotten about."

He gave his listener a frustrated smile. "You know, on one occasion here on the beach, I walked into the sea with my bucket and with the spade started to fill it with water."

- "You wanted to surround the sand-castle you had built with a mote?" said the sergeant quickly, proudly thinking that he had cleverly guessed what was coming next.

Roger left him both disappointed and dumbfounded. "Nope. I wanted to dig a hole in the ocean! And now I have the same sense of trying to do the impossible."

They had arrived at the hotel when the kindly police officer put his hand on the forlorn seeker's shoulder in a friendly fashion. He wished him luck and said that unfortunately he had to put an end to an agreeable chance meeting, put a stop to an unusual conversation, and head off home.

Apart from the twinge of regret that they had to part so soon, Jack also felt a dose of wonder at the fact that he should be undergoing such an emotion. He had, after all, only met Roger a few minutes ago. With all that, he was more hopeful as to the outcome to the plight of his newly found and quickly lost friend. He turned back suddenly after having taken a few paces into the night with his as yet silent companion.

- "Mr. Penrose," he said through the fog that was now creeping landward from the darkness of the open sea, "it suddenly occurred to me that it's more than likely you did see the person that you were looking for, and that after all these years you simply didn't recognize him – or her. Just a thought. Good night, sir."

Roger made his way up to his room musing on the policeman's last misty words. They certainly sounded reasonable. In fact, the more he thought about it, the more obvious they resulted.

"Of course," his mind went on saying as he got from his wet clothes into his dry pyjamas, hopped into the welcoming bed and buried himself beneath the blankets. "Of course; the people he had known as a kid on holiday would have changed completely. Hadn´t *he*? Even if he had known exactly who it was he had been searching for, they would probably be unrecognizable. Wasn´t *he?*"

With a sigh he turned to thinking about the pretty plain-clothes detective. She hadn´t spoken a word during all their time together, which was either bad manners or meant that she had some hidden reason for not doing so. Being strangers, what motive could she have for not speaking to him?

Roger then realized that her older companion hadn´t introduced her to him either. Jack was obviously a congenial fellow, which made his perplexity all the more acute. What could have caused him to deliberately act in such a way? As he began to imagine an array of ludicrous possibilities, he slowly fell under the dominion of another fantasy world commonly known of as sleep.

Chapter Two

Roger shook off its replenishing hold the next day at five o´clock sharp, just as he had done for the last decade and a half. He then went through his usual morning routine, which consisted of two things during the first hour or so; the first was a cup of good hot coffee, which on this occasion had to be skipped, finding himself as he was in a hotel. He thought about calling room-service but quickly dismissed the idea; apart from the bother, he in some way felt sure that he was taking the necessary first steps on a new road that would mean a change in his lifestyle.

The thought caused a shiver to reverberate through every cell in his body: it was the age-old fear of the unknown, of letting go and not being able to calculate the results of the free-fall. He had always based his decisions on imperative data, and even though an element of going on a hunch did make an appearance now and again, he had always felt safer in his world of logic, statistics and most important of all, routine. This brought him to what normally came after the preparation, and during the taking of, the missing coffee.

He opened the French windows of the spacious suite as much as they would allow, sat down in the armchair he had placed in front of them, wrapped himself in the blanket that he had taken from the bed and let the salty air blow over him in strong, unremitting gusts. He sat there in the dark, feeling the cold breeze flowing over his face and through his short, neatly cut hair, letting time go out of the window and allowing his imagination to fly through the clouds, impervious to all else. The silence reminded him that, at home, he would be listening to his favorite music, but he quickly shrugged off the absence as another step towards his as yet undiscovered future.

It suddenly dawned on him that, in all of his working years, this had been practically his only moment of intimacy, of distraction from his fervour for being available at any hour, at all hours; on any day, on all days. If the boss had ever needed a report on his desk first thing on Monday morning, he would be the one who volunteered to get it done, even if it meant being at the computer on the Jewish Sabbath and the Christian day of the Lord.

Yes, the almighty might have rested, but not Roger. If something urgent came up while he and half the staff were on holiday, he would gladly put a hurried end to his summer break; Christmas and New Year could, and would, be taken as the most ordinary of workdays if the need arose; and of course, he would always be busy at his desk when the rest of his colleagues began to stroll into the office, either on the darkest and coldest of winter mornings, or on the most pleasant of summer daybreaks.

Today, however, he felt a growing need for breaking every last one of those self-imposed rules and regulations. Indeed, he was now looking forward to it with an almost child-like enthusiasm.

When he finally opened his eyes once more, he looked at his watch and was surprised to see that it was near on seven o′clock. After the unusually long escape from reality (or towards it, as he sometimes speculated), he decided that it was now time for that coffee. "The sunlight will soon be flooding the beach with its welcomed rays," he said aloud to the now red-tinted horizon. "The dining room will soon be open to a host of hungry "*holidayers*" in search of nourishment, before carrying on with their holidaying day." Just like the evening before, his previously unknown locutionary prowess made him smile.

As he did so he looked into the full-length looking glass that stood in a corner to the left of the balcony doors. He burst out laughing while saying to the reflection, "Hey, maybe I should use my newly found talent to keep a diary of my newly found life."

With that enticing thought, he made his way towards the bathroom, which was right beside the front door. He was surprised to see a rectangular form at its base. He reached it in a couple of strides and saw that someone had slipped a postcard under the door. Intrigued, he bent down and picked it up. The photo was the same as the one on the postcard that he had written the night before. He turned it over.

"Well, I´ll be….", he blurted out, "it *is* the same one. It´s mine. What the…?"

He cut his own expression short when he read over the message he had written, and then glanced at the address; he was stunned to see that he was the addressee.

"But how did it get...?"

He stopped in his verbal tracks once more. Before the question had been finished, Roger had already guessed the answer.

He slowly leaned his back against the door while his agile mind came to an astonishing conclusion. Here in his hands, surely thanks to Jack, was the first clue as to what he might be doing here in the town of so many happy childhood recollections; it wasn't a search for some friend or other. No, he was looking for the boy who had had the privilege to live those wonderful moments!

The dumbstruck financial wizard strolled back to the open windows where, instead of closing them, he looked down at the glistening scene below and was immediately transformed into the youngster he was seemingly searching for.

The seafront had suddenly become memory lane as he walked along for a bit before turning right into the street that led uphill to a small shop which sold all types of articles that were needed daily. Most days he would go to buy bread on a morning just like this one; and every now and then, if he had the luck of being given a couple of pennies, either from his parents or even from a friend, he would excitedly visit the welcoming establishment with the sole idea of buying the only licorice flavored toffees to be found anywhere within the confines of his little world.

Then he was walking along, talking and laughing with some mates –as well as chewing with relish the treasured sweets. As usual, at least in his flashbacks, the sun was generously pouring down the exact amount of light and warmth that made perfect the days for doing anything, and everything, that a group of kids might decide to do.

And do they did; endlessly and tirelessly absorbing the emotions that filled them with the joy of life, like a plant that absorbs the rays that made it all possible.

Still enjoying the exquisite taste that the caramels offered, they were now walking along the steel tracks of a railway line, either going somewhere or coming back from another place. It didn't matter in the slightest; they were nothing more than a small gang of friends with nothing more to do than…. nothing in particular; nowhere to go except…. no place in especial.

Whatever Roger did and wherever he went, accompanied or not, the only thing of importance was the feeling of living in a world of magic, of never-ending happiness.

The thirty-five-year-old was now standing once more back in the present as the images receded into the distant past. He exhaled a sigh full of nostalgia, before asking himself the obvious question: what about the bad moments? And the cold rainy days?

All of the uncomfortable experiences that he had obviously had to live through were, for the moment at least, left aside. He made no effort to recall anything along those lines.

- "Well,", he said to himself and the world that filled his view, "I'm not here to look for such things, am I? So, let's get to it without further delay!"

Chapter Three

It was just after mid-day when Roger had come to sit at an outdoor table of a waterfront café. The wind had died momentarily, there wasn't a cloud to be seen, and the timid spring sun was now warming to the task of turning today into a pleasant one, as pleasing had been his stroll around the port observing the recently arrived fishermen going about their tasks; some unloading the catch, some attending to the cleaning and mending of the tools of their craft, and all seemingly unconscious of the hullabaloo of hungry birds above their heads.

He admired the courage of these men going out to sea in the black of night. A great deal of that respect stemmed from his phobia of the sea at any time, and in any weather, but the idea of being out there in the middle of that immensity of darkness with nothing but the opaque depths below his feet was something that produced a feeling of horror of indescribable proportions.

The waitress came and went; so, while waiting for her to return with the desired eatables and drinkables, he took out the postcard and looked at it anew. He began the inevitable self-interrogation: "but haven't I achieved exactly what I set out to do? Didn't I work like a dog for fifteen years so that I no longer have to work again in any way, shape or form? Am I not akin to a gladiator who fights and fights until he, at last, conquers his right to be where I am right now; in a situation that means that I no longer have to carry on doing anything except what my heart desires? And does that not mean that I should automatically be full of joy? How many others could say the same about their situation? Isn´t the world my oyster? Wouldn´t those hard-working fishermen give anything to find the pearl that I now hold in my keeping?"

Apparently, it wasn´t the case! The postcard was simply an outward symptom of the malaise he now knew to be suffering. It was becoming obvious that he was only at the outset of his undefined and as yet undefinable quest - not at the end of it.

He felt a little downhearted, asking himself as to the how and where to start. He corrected himself straightaway. The ´where´ was obviously here, for some reason that escaped him. The town where he had spent most of his years growing up would have been more logical, surely. In any case, he told himself mournfully, it was beyond any doubt that the search was doomed to failure: that kid was gone forever; he was no more than a phantom, a ghost in his mind. And of course, he couldn´t *be* five, or eight, or ten years old again, or go around acting as if he were. That in itself was a childish thought.

The vexing piece of cardboard was let fall heedlessly on the table. He closed his eyes as his head began to swirl like the flapping, boisterous birds above the quaint quay. He wasn´t used to so much ´philosophizing´, as he put it, never having seen any practical use for it.

A sudden darkness crossed his face. "It´s got you wandering then, hasn´t it, Mr. Penrose?"

Roger, startled out of his musing, immediately opened his eyes and looked up at the owner of the shadow and the voice therein. He greeted the suited figure with genuine delight. Could it be that he was already missing the almost permanent and unavoidable contact with others? Was he already suffering from having endless time on his hands? He had never been one for idly sitting around either, although it had to be said that spare time hadn´t been a luxury that he had ever had the occasion to get used to. Now he was facing the challenge of learning how to enjoy and make the most of it.

- "Jack, great to see you again," he said, getting to his feet and shaking the likable policeman´s hand. "And I told you last night, call me Roger please, even if and when you are dutifully maintaining the peace on the streets. Anyhow, the answer to your question is no - I do suppose you are referring to the postcard. Well, I haven´t given it the slightest thought. My mind was engaged in trying to fathom out how many seagulls it takes to make a flock." Exactly as he had done on their memorable meeting the night before, he pointed to the scene above the fishermen´s heads as the incontestable proof of his words.

It was Jack´s turn to discourteously ignore the wisecrack. He stood looking down at the jester with a face that looked as if it had been recently quarried.

- "Really truly," Roger went on, feigning innocence. "Hold on a minute; you´re not suggesting some deep and subtle meaning regarding the fact that the written to, and the writer of this postcard, are one and the same person, are you? Nonsense! It was no more than a lapse."

His last affirmation didn´t convince either of the two. - "As you wish, Roger," Jack calmly replied, "I don´t mean to intrude by any means but allow me to say by way of some friendly, and professional advice, that if you ever find yourself in the police interrogation room, you´ll have to be more persuasive in your declaration." He then wisely broke the tension with an amiable, "Having lunch, are we?"

- "You are absolutely correct," was the relieved reply. "*We* are! Take a seat and join me. After your courteous behavior last night, the least I can do is to invite you to something."

The proposal was gladly accepted. For one thing, it was a good excuse for the sergeant to rest the feet that had taken him for a two-hour non-stop stroll since he had gone on duty. Secondly, in the few minutes that the regulations allowed, they could begin to get to know one another a little more. Roger had openly told him a little of his life, so Jack cautiously began to tell a little of his own.

He had always longed to be, and had always been, a police officer. He possessed the admirable attitude of wanting to make his town a decent place for people to go about their business and get on with their lives as pleasantly and orderly as he could possibly make it. Modern policing, he went on to explain –without going into details- had changed since he was a cadet, of course, but that fact couldn´t take away the twinge of regret that he felt with respect to his soon to be retirement from the force.

- "I´ll be leaving things in good hands, nonetheless," he said, finishing his brief introduction.

- "Ah yes," Roger said with unforeseen enthusiasm, "your charming partner from last night, I take it you mean. The silent flower of the law... I do hope she's tougher than she looks."

- "Just you try messing with her and you'll find out quick enough. And as for her silence, I think that last night was one of the few times I've seen her so timid. Not like her at all, in fact."

- "My fault probably," Roger interrupted. "It was a rather strange scene that played host to our first encounter. I hope the second will be a little more orthodox. Isn't she with you by the way?"

- "No, being a plain-clothes detective, she doesn't go around with me. We only coincided last night on our way home together."

Jack had given his explanation as naturally as anyone might do when talking about the weather, or the price of carrots, but the younger man's look of shock forced him to see his words from a different perspective; namely, the perverted conclusion that he supposed Roger to have reached. He couldn't resist a little leg pulling, however.

- "Well after all, you did say that she's an attractive woman, didn't you," the policeman continued nonchalantly. "And what's more, in the days we live in, I'm surprised that you are so scandalized. Or is it that you're slightly jealous?" he finished with as straight a face as he could manage.

Roger tried to wriggle his way out of the uncomfortable situation in which he found himself -and imagined Jack to be in- with more absurd denials. He might have been a stock market whiz-kid, but at that moment he was acting no better than a silly child. Jack, once again, wasn't to be fooled.

- "Young man," went on the police officer in a tone of gently delivered reprimand, "if our newfound friendship is to last longer than the time it takes to finish this cup of tea, then you really must be more sincere."

The retired broker was muted; lost as to how to react to the unexpected words of the soon to be retired police sergeant. These might well be 'modern times', as Jack had pointed out, but the benign image he had formed of him began to fade.

Not only is the old guy living with a woman half his age, he was thinking, *he has no qualms about turning it into a laughing matter.* He decided to take Jack's advice on being frank, break his silence and give voice his to his indignation. Happily, for him, it turned out that he was unable to do so.

He had never believed much in good fortune – a well thought out strategy was, for him, the best way to a fortunate outcome – but, on this occasion, lady luck manifested herself in the flesh, stepping in to stop him from opening his mouth and, therefore, making a monumental mistake: at that precise moment, the lady in question appeared walking towards him in a bright yellow dress and mauve cardigan. Her chestnut hair fell in waves onto the shoulders that gracefully carried the colorful attire while she was talking into the ear of another woman who was walking alongside her.

Her companion was of roughly the same age, just slightly smaller in height, and only slightly plainer in looks, as well as in the way she was clothed – in Roger's opinion at any rate. The most outstanding feature of the newcomer was the long straight blonde hair trailing behind her, carried upon the sea breeze.

The fact of the matter is that if the two women had arrived from the opposite direction, then he wouldn't have seen them on time; he would have loosened his tongue, and all would most probably have been lost with respect to the friendship that he would hopefully strike up with Jack – and maybe with someone else too.

Roger's gaze was fixed on the taller of the two women. He pursed his lips as he watched her approach with a smoothly swaying elegance, lay a hand delicately on Jack's right shoulder and present him with an affectionate kiss on the left cheek.

- "Hi dad, I see that your path and that of last night's stranger have crossed again," she said with a voice that Roger might have described in his future diary as suggestive. She finished in a whisper. "Is he asleep, or meditating? Or doesn't he wish to see me?"

On hearing how she had greeted the man that he had been about to unfairly scold, Roger had sunk back into his chair, allowing his eyelids to shut out the world in the process. It was he himself who both gave and received the reprimand.

- "My god," began the mental self-infliction, "I had spoken to him only moments before about having a second chance to present myself to the lady under more favorable circumstances… and there she is, standing right in front of me, most likely thinking that I'm the weirdest guy on the planet."

- "No, my dear," the father answered softly, "He's recovering from conclusion jumping, although in all fairness it might be said that it is in part my fault. Let's just say, however, that he's more than a little surprised to find out that you and I have such a close relationship and leave it at that."

A pair of sparkling brown eyes were found to be looking directly into those of Roger's when he plucked up the courage to open them again.

- "Hello," the brightly dressed lady greeted him, "our family and professional ties do take a lot of people by surprise, although I don't rightly understand why. Not to worry, though. One of those unsolved mysteries. What would life be without them?" were the first words that she had spoken directly to him -and in an ironic tone that he would soon become familiar with. "But let me make amends for my strange and silent behavior last night," she went on, now brandishing the cheekiest and most unrestrained of smiles. "My name is Lilian. And this is my friend Cynthia, also known to the chosen few as Alex."

Roger stood up, quickly recovering his composure. He greeted Cynthia in a polite fashion before turning again to her floral companion, shaking her slender hand and apologizing in turn for his own queer conduct, both today and the evening before.

- "You've changed since yesterday," he said, indicating with his eyes her colorful clothing and loosely falling hair, both so different from what she had been wearing on their first encounter. Then he went on to explain the pleasant surprise he had felt on hearing her name. "Do you know, I was thinking to myself as you approached that you gave the impression of looking just like a pretty water-lily floating elegantly on the water."

- "That's a very beautiful and poetic compliment for any woman to receive," she replied, blushing slightly, which only added to the effect, "but I'm still the same person you met yesterday. And I hope you won't take it as an offence if I say that you don't seem to have changed. *My impression* is that you are still as mad as a hatter."

Roger tried to take her surprisingly frank affirmation as no more than a harmless, whimsical phrase.

- "Absolutely not," he retorted jovially, "although you're totally wrong about me. In fact, I saw myself in the mirror this morning; just plain old me."

- "Plain old me, that's a good one," Jack had begun saying after his daughter and Cynthia had accepted his invitation to join them. He had beaten Roger to it, although it wouldn't be too far from the truth to say that his good-mannered behavior was also an excellent pretext for breaking the initial contact between the two who still stood before him with hands clasped and eyes locked together after a length of time, as he saw it, more than prudent. "Here comes the waitress. Take a seat and a menu, ladies," he almost commanded.

The signs of mutual attraction were more than obvious to him, and in his role as the protective father, the idea didn't overly please him. Roger was a passerby. Irrespective of the friendship they had begun, and for as much as he might feel a good deal of empathy with the man and his dilemma, he wasn't going to permit his daughter to be hurt by a weekend romance. He knew, certainly, that he couldn't stop the inevitable if it were to happen, but his character wouldn't allow him to sit sipping tea while events unfolded before his eyes. He continued.

- "Well then, plain old Roger, will you be heading back to your home-town soon? And what *do* you think about the now famous postcard?"

Roger saw nothing ulterior in the allusion to his possible prompt departure, or at least he made no sign of having done so. He limited himself to explaining that his original plans had been to stay for the weekend, but that he was now considering the idea of extending his visit for a few days more. The experienced policeman's gaze was scrutinizing Roger's body movements so that the almost imperceptible flash of his eyes towards Lilian as he ended the phrase didn't go unnoticed. The first to react to Roger's disclosure was, surprisingly, the younger of the two women present.

- "Great, I can show you the prettiest place in the town. I mean the zoo, naturally; I was on my way there after picking up my laptop from the repair shop. Apart from the animals, there are also beautiful lawns with flowers coming into bloom, as well as the wonders to be found in the botanical gardens. I should know: I look after it all!"

- "Don't be absurd, Alex," said Lilian, ill-manneredly admonishing her friend for the suggestion. "Mr. Penrose is not here to get anywhere near those smelly animals in the zoo, and I'm sure he doesn't want to spend the day in amongst your flowers; he's a big city boy."

- "No, you judge me wrongly again, Lilian. I'll gratefully accept the offer. As a matter of fact, I think it's a great idea," he said, genuinely delighted. As a kid he had always loved spending time in the zoo looking at the exotic animals, especially the gorillas. "But what do you look after Cynthia, the flora or the fauna?"

- "The plants. I'm a gardener!" she replied proudly.

- "So why don't we all three of us go and make a day of it," Roger proposed. "With Lilian's father's permission, of course."

The idea of someone asking for permission to take his daughter for an outing tickled Jack. He was well aware that Roger wasn't being serious, but he also knew that the old-fashioned chivalry was feigned in a goodhearted fashion, with no kind of sarcasm involved, which is why, for as silly as it would seem for the unimportance of the comment, his old heart was touched. Nowadays people would call him 'sentimental', whereas in years gone by and never to return, the term would have been 'big softy'; but in either case he didn't care, that was the way he was.

Roger, meanwhile, was busy keeping well-hidden his disappointment at Lilian's firm refusal. Wild humans should be behind bars, not wild animals, she was saying with a metaphor that well suited her occupation. She delighted in being witness to the first, and abhorred the second, she added with a certain self-satisfaction that might easily have passed for conceit. Indeed, from the expression on her face and the apparent ring in her voice, Roger surmised that she encountered her work highly gratifying, but was taken aback a little by her virulent attack on the zoos; from which he also concluded that her father was obviously not joking when he had advised him that she was sterner than the attractive, but slender figure that had aroused his attention.

He agreed in principle with her stance on encaging animals. He himself had never had as much as a hamster, and the idea of a bird locked in a cage unable to spread its wings he thought barbarous. Notwithstanding, he was always the pragmatist: as long as the wild beasts were imprisoned, they would have to be looked after, so why not allow the public to enjoy them while they may. After all, they couldn't simply be shipped back and let loose in the jungles of the world where they would almost certainly die of hunger or fall easy prey to predators accustomed to a life that the zoo animals knew nothing of. Cynthia expressed a similar opinion.

- "In a few years, they will have disappeared for the most part, as the zoos close down when the animals in them die of natural causes. The important thing is that no more are brought out of the wild to replace them. Our own plans are to let it run down slowly until it eventually becomes nothing more, and nothing less, than a huge park full of trees, grass, and flowers of all kinds. Not to mention the indigenous population of birds and small animals." She knew of other plans that had been drawn up for some of the enclosed animals, but as they had never been confirmed, she didn't think it the right moment to disclose them.

Jack and Roger raised their teacups and toasted Cynthia's discourse while Lilian remained adamant, flatly refusing to go anywhere near the place. So, as it turned out, the on-duty officer continued with his rounds, while Roger went sightseeing with the green-fingered young lady instead of with her hardheaded friend.

Chapter Four

"Well then, Cynthia," began Roger lightheartedly, shaking off the frustration of having had to watch Lilian drift slowly, and yet to his mind, reluctantly away -in spite of her speech. "How do we get there; is it far?"

He seemed to remember taking the bus to the zoo as a kid with his parents while on vacations here in the town, but the distance in time clouded his memories of the distance in space. To his delight, the young woman told him that he was going to have the chance once again to relive his childhood ride, courtesy of the public transport system. The stop was right beside where they were, that being the reason, she hurriedly clarified, for making her and her friend's appearance at the place of the chance meeting.

Shortly after the sound of the engine that accelerated the bus forward had died to a low hum, Jack's sight was called urgently to attention by a familiar display of bright colors, directly falling on Lilian's elegant form as she stood casually looking at the wears presented in a jewelry store. He was unable to abandon the spectacle, obliging first his eyes, then his head to swivel and turn until they could no longer do so.

Cynthia was busy with her smartphone, not unlike most of the others who were sharing the bus with them, all seemingly oblivious to anything else that might be happening around them. She finally closed the case and apologized to her fellow passenger with a smile that conveyed her mildly felt embarrassment at not being the good-mannered hostess.

Roger, especially in the line of work that had taken up fifteen hectic years of his life, had been addicted to the electronic device more than most, so that he was naturally understanding in his acceptance of the apology. In any case, he said to her softly, it wasn't for him to propose an amendment to the use of the things, or the people who spent their time playing with them. As part of his endeavor to take a new path, he had made a point of not bringing his own phone with him to the beach, although he admitted to feeling a little like a gunslinger without his Colt 45 in its holster - but neither was he in any kind of danger, was he? The young woman maintained a straight face, and a closed mouth.

"If anyone feels the need to contact me, let them send a postcard," he finished with a jest, although the wry smile it produced disappeared in the act of clapping his forehead; his postcard was lying where he had left it on the table of the café where he had lunched.

Cynthia's only reaction was to ask a simple, succinct question, with no fuss whatsoever.

"What's the matter, Roger?"

"Maybe it's a consequence of my new relaxed attitude, but I'm afraid we'll have to get off at the next stop and take another bus back to where we met. I've left something of importance there."

"You wouldn't mean this, by any chance?" she asked, calmly holding up what she had considerately rescued from being abandoned. The thing seemed to have a life of its own, going from one person's care to another's – and yet, always returning to whom it belonged. The truth is she had planned on surprising Roger with it sometime later that day.

The young woman promptly stood up. "This is our stop. We're just a short walk away from my place of work; or should I say my workshop? I'm an artist, you know," she finished proudly as they stepped down from the bus.

They were standing on the pavement of a quiet road about a mile outside of town, with a dirt pathway before their feet that headed into typically British woodland. After some fifty or so feet, it bent towards the left and was lost to sight amongst the trees and shrubbery. Roger was thrilled.

"But I thought we were going to the zoo. Or is it a safari park?"

"I thought you might enjoy the walk, and this track leads to a back gate for which I have the key. Mind your step."

"This is truly magical. What a great idea it was bringing me this way."

He was already on his way as he spoke, overcome by a child-like impulsiveness. On reaching the bend visible from the roadside, he turned to see that Cynthia was standing in the same spot, calmly observing the 'little boy' skipping along the trail.

"What are you waiting for?" he shouted out impatiently to her.

She was thinking that the melancholy that had descended on him the night before, according to Lilian's evaluation, had vanished along with the rain. Neither of them were as yet aware that all the consequences hadn't, for before Cynthia had covered the distance between them, the impetuous young man made an about turn as if to carry on and stepped full into a puddle left by the weather's bothersome self-indulgence.

"I know I shouldn't say it, but I did tell you to be careful!" were the words that reached Roger's ears, amidst the accompanying naughty school-girl giggles. "Why don't you hold on a second and let me be your pathfinder."

After a few twists and turns along the track, Roger's demeanor turned from playful to more serious one. He had always been of the timid sort when it came to personal relationships, so he found it hard to pluck up the courage to ask Cynthia's view of another woman. Impelled by the burning desire to know, he tried to approach the matter with an air of nonchalance.

"So, tell me," he said, picking up a pebble from the ground and throwing it into the undergrowth, "how is it that you and Lilian, a gardener and a police detective, became acquainted?"

The story he heard was fascinating. She described the details of a murder case that the police had been investigating, and of how she had received a visit one day from a couple of plain clothes detectives, asking for her help in identifying a plant found in the victim's hand. It turned out to be a rare species, not native to Britain, and grown only under very particular conditions. Her botanical knowledge was to be one of the keys in wrapping up the case, or so the police department hoped.

"Then you are also a crime-buster! I am impressed," said Roger, "That's quite a story. And one of the officers in question was Lilian, I take it."

"Indeed," she answered in a rueful tone, "One of the officers in question was Lilian, although I must point out that in the end the case was never resolved."

"You don't sound too enthusiastic about it all. Stop me if you think I'm being overly intrusive, but is it because of the outcome of the case, or is there something you haven't told me about your relationship? Do you have a problem with her? What is she like?"

He told himself with relief that he had finally gotten round to asking what he really wanted to know, although his satisfaction lasted no longer than the few seconds it took for him to realize that the ensuing silence was the only response that he would receive by way of an answer.

In effect, they walked the rest of the way without a word, making him feel a little awkward. It soon melted away, however, as he gradually paid attention to what was going on around them. His senses were being treated to the spectacle of nature's provocative array: his eyes were penetrated by a shady greenish light that lit the surrounding air; ears delighted by the choir of woodland birdsong; sense of smell inundated by the aroma of the lush damp undergrowth.

The wild scenery changed when the unruffled Cynthia turned the key that unlocked the gate she had mentioned, now passing through what signaled the end of nature's uninhibited exuberance and the beginning of the tamed beauty of finely cut lawns and strategically placed flowerbeds, not to mention the duck-filled ponds. Needless to say, it always struck Cynthia as equally beautiful.

"Welcome to my Garden of Eden," she said with a broad sweep of her arm.

Roger was in no position to disagree, but he did have a question to ask, something that had always nagged at his mind.

"I wonder why people feel the need to put nature into geometrical order, and why they find it so pleasing to look upon. You are the one responsible for this particular little paradise; why the necessity of taking chaos and putting it under strict control?"

"In the first place, order has always come from chaos. And secondly, the forest may look anarchic to you, but I assure you that it isn't at all disorganized. Everything in it is exactly as it should be. And that implies order - or design!"

The surprise that caught hold of Roger's placid semblance forced his eyebrows to raise themselves like a drawbridge, allowing the passage of a newly forming image of the woman beside him. The question he had formulated had been more than a little rhetorical, so he hadn't really expected an answer of any sort - and certainly not one so eloquent. She returned his gaze steadily, along with a smile that said, *'I know something that you don't, and that you'll have to find out for yourself: if you are interested'*.

Then she raised her harm once again. "Well then, my office is on the other side of that hill. You can´t see from here, but it´s right next to the greenhouses that make up the botanical gardens."

The pointing finger used to indicate the whereabouts of her ´headquarters´, then moved from ten minutes past the hour to ten minutes to, she being the hourly reference point. "On the other hand, the entrance to the zoo is over that way; which do you prefer to see first?"

"You said that you were going to be my guide. Lead on."

It was a fair distance to the long-standing greenhouses designed and built in Victorian times, so an excess of trudging limited them to the briefest of visits. Roger showed himself to be the lesser fit of the two, thus the pair of weary legs that were outstretched before the bench where they were soon sitting comfortably on. It was conveniently situated in the shade of a weeping willow, lending the pair´s pale skins protection from the unusually warm spring sun. The tour of the Botanical Gardens could wait.

The bench came complete with a table made from thick wooden trunks that were skillfully cut and smoothed, so as to serve as a pleasant picnic area. Yet another attribute to the chosen spot was the fact that it faced a small lake inhabited by a few ducks and some moorhens.

What specially caught Roger's eye, nonetheless, was a majestic mass of waterlilies floating radiantly on the far side of the pond. He was admiring their vivacious presence when Cynthia's sweet tones delicately severed the momentary harmony between observer and observed, between the thinker and the thought of.

"A gorgeous flower."

"Yes."

"But... how to reach it without drowning?"

"Is this a Koan? Or a common everyday type of riddle; the kind that has an answer, I mean? In any case, isn't entering the water prohibited?"

At that moment, he raised his sight so as to look beyond the lake, back to the lawn that went sloping up to the forest whose paths served Cynthia as a private entrance. Amidst the short grass, and under the scrutiny of a handful of ash trees, he saw carefully placed beds of a bulbous, mostly purple colored flower, whose name lay outside the knowledge of the city boy.

He knew of the waterlilies, as they had been present in the small artificial pond of a colleague from his past life, but he had to ask the expert what this new species was.

"In the case of you ever having the inclination to do so, I first of all have to advise you that it is one that you would have to be careful handling. It's toxic!"

"Is that so? Then it's lucky I have a guide with me, isn't it?"

"That depends on the guide, doesn't it? Anyway, to other things. Tell me something about yourself apart from the little I learned from Lilian: namely, that you're a self-retired wheeler dealer who is on a visit to his childhood holiday resort, and that you're looking for the shameless little urchin who left you with ice-cream on your face before running out, never to be seen again. Am I right?"

Roger laughed at the memory while pulling in his legs and twisting round to face the woman responsible for the peaceful environment that surrounded them. He knew, however, that there was more to his laid-back disposition than just the beautiful designer gardens; the designer's mere presence made him feel relaxed and comfortable.

"I'm not a mind reader," she said softly, "you'll have to use your vocal cords to communicate with me."

"Sorry Cynthia, I'm just so taken with this place. Now, I'm going to answer your question with complete sincerity, something I haven't done with Jack - as yet. But allow me to ask you something first. Why do he and Lilian call you Alex? And why do you give me the impression of being something more than your everyday, run-of-the-mill gardener."

"I asked first," she said with gentle reproach. "However, as a reward for your generous words, I'll respond to both questions with one and the same answer."

It seemed that ´Alex´ was the diminutive of Alexandria, the city that had been the custodian of so much human sapience, accumulated throughout so many centuries, millennium even, from all parts of the world, and tragically destroyed overnight, prey to the consuming flames of human folly. The relation between the ancient city and the present-day parkland caretaker didn´t become clear until the creative gardener calmly explained, as if it were a mere nothing, that she hadn´t always been such.

"You see, before I began to look after all that you can see, I was a philosopher."

"My goodness," Roger let out, flabbergasted, "I'm in conversation with a sage? This is far out. So, what happened? How did it come about that you went from having your head floating in the clouds to burying your hands in the earth?"

"No, no," she said firmly," I answered your question, so now it´s your turn. If you are very lucky, and if you ever stay around long enough, it might possibly be that I'll tell you how to handle those poisonous flowers over there beyond the water lilies, as well as telling you about my change of heading. So, please get to it!"

"First let me elaborate on what I was getting at a moment ago: I've paraded a misleading idea about myself to Jack and Lilian."

"You have a funny way of expressing yourself, and you cleverly avoided using the word 'lie', but carry on."

"It wasn't exactly a lie, Cynthia. What I told them was what should have been the truth, and would have been, if it wasn't for one small weakness in my plans. Let me quickly say that all the events are as I told your friends. The thing is, I haven't completed the goal yet."

"Are you saying you haven't retired?

"You are clever, aren't you?

"Very much so. But tell me, who or what is the impediment?"

"*I am.* When the moment of glory arrived six months ago, I was betrayed by my own cowardice, to the point of being unable to hand in my notice. What I did instead was to ask for a sabbatical year. I gave the excuse of needing to recharge my batteries, that sort of thing." He ended his confession looking at his soiled footwear making a small rut in the ground.

"Now, now, Mr. Penrose, self-pity doesn't work with me," she said playfully, "and neither can I allow so much self-reproach. You suffered a little 'vertigo', shall we say. I imagine that in your line of work you would have handled stressful situations almost on a daily basis, but perhaps you had never come face to face with pure, raw fear before then."

"I did once, as a matter of fact, here on the beach. I was playing football with my dad when he kicked the ball out into the water and I ran in after it, with such enthusiasm that I waded a little too far before he could warn me of what was about to happen; the sea bottom fell suddenly away, I lost my footing and a wave took me under. All at once, I was engulfed in darkness. I only remember feeling that I was a thousand feet below the surface with no hope of getting back. Ever since then I suffer from an uncontrollable phobia of the sea, if you'll excuse the redundancy."

"That's why you couldn't hand in your notice: the fear of losing your feet again, of finding yourself without the solid, comfortable security that your job furnishes you with. Let me put another question to you. Could you swim at the time of the accident?"

"Yes, but why do you ask?"

"Well, you panicked in the water in spite of being able to swim, and you also panicked in the office, even though you know that your retirement is well taken care of money-wise. So, it's vitally important that you overcome the incident with your resignation, get back there as soon as possible, and start bidding farewell; firmly, calmly, and definitively. If you still want to carry on with the idea, that is."

There followed a pause in which the effects of re-living past traumas were evident from the anxious expression that had taken residence on Roger's face. Cynthia kindly decided to draw his thoughts away from the distressing memories by getting straight to the heart of the debate: what motives did he have for wanting to give up working at such a young age?

The only answer he had to offer was that he wanted 'to find happiness'. He felt sure that Cynthia must think him the most naïve creature she had come across, although, fortunately for him, it wasn't the case. She carried serenely on.

"Well, I think that your act of sincerity brings us nicely to what intrigued me ever since I heard it from Lilian's lips. To the point of me inviting you here, if the truth be told. I'm referring, of course, to the piece of cardboard that I rescued from the café table."

"What's your interpretation? Roger asked, half joking and half serious. "What words of wisdom can you give me?"

"You thought that by doing what you did – albeit on a trial basis - you would now be wealthy, carefree, and able to do whatever you wanted in life. You just said so yourself, correct? Now you are finding out that happiness isn't an automatic consequence of your actions. One outcome you certainly never expected was your trip here and the postcard wishing that the child you were was here. Except that, in my *unalterable* opinion, you aren't looking for that little boy!"

"No?"

"Not at all.

"Well, I'll be damned.

"Cheer up; all is not yet lost. Your quest isn't to *be* the boy again: it's all about being as happy now as you were when you were the boy."

"So," Roger asked in a tone that struck Cynthia as self-mockery, "where do I start, then?"

"In my opinion, we should start by making our way across to the zoo. In that way I can keep my promise of showing you around and at the same time we can shake off the shackles of this heavy conversation for a while."

Roger suggested they leave the animals for the following day, as it was getting a little late to visit them in the manner that they deserved. A better idea, he continued, would be take a walk around the lake and then on up to the exit that opened onto the woods; and, he thought to himself, maybe she could provide him with some answers.

They made their way along the lakeside enjoying the more than pleasant afternoon. Cynthia had at the same time taken off her shoes and was relishing the sensation of the still moist grass under her bare feet, while the lapping of the water against the shore and the noisy quacking of the ducks were enjoyed with her eyes almost closed and an enigmatic smile on her face. She suddenly stopped.

The financial wizard was expectant; for the first time since they had met this morning she had a serious expression on her face, which he supposed would mean a renewing of their deep conversation. At that moment, with his spirits on the up, he couldn't imagine how wrong he was.

"I beg your pardon," he retorted perplexed, unable to make head or tail of what she had just asked him.

"The Ancient Egyptians. They had no word for death. Don't you find that fascinating?"

"Eh… well... I suppose so. But what's that got to do with anything?"

The sun, momentarily hidden behind the outlier of a horde of clouds that would soon conquer the blue skies, shone again, as did Cynthia's smile. Without a word, she started running ahead.

At this point Roger was completely bewildered; had she just made fun of him and insolently left him in ridicule?

Alex had come to a halt and was now looking back at Roger with the same self-assuredness that had accompanied her throughout the day.

"What are you waiting for? Are you just going to stand there for the rest of the afternoon? If you don't move soon, I'll never be able to comply with your request."

Now he was sure that she was playing games with him, so he strode towards her intent on putting an end to her behaving like an impertinent child. Roger wasn't one for such time-wasting.

"Now listen here Cynthia, if you are going to go on behaving like a little girl, or if you want to continue making fun of me, then I'd kindly ask you to let me know so that we can simply go back to town and call it a day!"

He immediately felt that he had been too harsh on her and tried to make amends – if it was still possible.

"A day to be remembered, certainly," was his bungling attempt at fixing the mess that he was causing.

Cynthia had indeed lost the cheerful semblance that she had so far demonstrated, although she wasn't upset; it was more a sense of disappointment. The chances of finding someone who understands us is like expecting to come across a diamond in a coal mine. She knew that her failure at not being prepared for his reaction was due to her foolish hope that it would be so nice to stumble on one.

"You really are a sober type, aren't you? And clumsy with it; I did warn you about handling certain plants, although I'm sure you haven't got a clue what I'm talking about."

"I'm sorry if I was rude," replied the embarrassed financer, not catching the meaning of Cynthia's cryptic words. "I thought that you were having me on, and I felt foolish. The truth is that it's something I've never tolerated. If it's any comfort, in your case I honestly hope you will accept my apology."

"Not to worry Roger. I'm pleased by your obvious sincerity, so let me tell you that what you perceived was not in any way intended. But there you have it; I can't control people's reactions, only take note and act in consequence."

"You are totally right about my being serious, Cynthia; only several months ago one of our habitual clients went so far as to tell me right to my face that I was "more solemn than the Old Testament." It's something I need to change and I'd like you to help me; I would dearly love for us to be friends!"

"Then call me Alex," she said cheerfully, shrugging off all remnants of bitterness. "Remember, however, that the next time you judge me, the courtroom will be adjourned until further notice."

Then she ran off again, all the way around the northern side of the lake, disappearing and emerging once more from behind the rushes and promptly throwing herself onto the grass between the water and the lovely purple plants, gasping for breath while waving to him.

She wasn't making fun of him at all, he realized. She was testing him; and he'd better pass the exam with an A plus. So, either on impulse or intuition, he took off his own shoes, waved back at her and then started to follow her unclad footsteps. When he reached her, she was now sitting on a white semi-circular stone bench not unlike the type of things he had seen in movies about Ancient Greece, obviously another of the landscaper's artistic touches.

"Well then Cynthia, I'd love for you to tell me about those lovely flowers behind you, but I think we should be heading homeward. Back to town, I mean to say. Come on, how about you and I replenishing our stores of energy with something to eat."

He was left a little disappointed (it seemed to be the tonic of the day) when she declined his offer, saying that with what looked like a storm brewing, she would have to stay a while to give some instructions to the groundkeepers that couldn´t wait for the next day. She would open the gate for him and the journey back was straightforward, as there was only one bus that passed where the woodland track met the tarmac.

Before she locked the gate behind him, he reminded her that he would be paying a visit to the zoo the next day and that he would be pleased if she could show him around.

"Don´t let your expectations of tomorrow spoil today´s fun. Every day brings a surprise, and you mustn´t spoil it by trying to anticipate it. Let it come as it will."

Roger asked himself if her words were more advice to help him on his quest, or an elegantly subtle form of saying ´no thanks´ for the second time in scarce minutes. Either way, once the philosopheress had turned away and said her goodbyes with a lackadaisical movement of her elegant hand, he decided that he would indeed forget future events and enjoy the stroll through the forest with no more on his mind than once again enjoying the sights and sounds it had to offer.

Before he took his first steps on his return journey, he had to ask something that if he didn´t, wouldn´t allow him to enjoy to the full the marvelous spectacle. Cynthia, already with her back towards Roger as she set out to settle the untold affairs, turned to face him with a smile that denoted her apparent delight at having her name called.

"Yes?" she said with provocative assuredness.

"Eh... don't you think it highly imprudent to have walked through an isolated forest with a man you had met only an hour before?"

"The day I can't act upon my own judgment of character," she replied as if she were talking to a young student, "is the day I'll go and live as a hermit."

Chapter Five

<Naughtily blows the gusting wind through my neatly and tidily combed crop of hair, bearing witness to this my first ever diary, in which I hope to tell, in my own particularly rebellious grammatical style, the story of my new life. I was yesterday told, notwithstanding, that I should get back home by the seemingly all-withstanding Cynthia. She, the philosopheress and the strange gardener; floral artist and sweet, serene sage. I also spoke alone, for the first time, to her alter ego, the beautiful, but so far impenetrable, Lilian.>

At that moment, the pencil that he had bought the night before, along with the diary he had promised to keep, broke; the memory of his short talk with the detective the evening before had come back to unsettle him. What added to his discomfort was the fact that he didn't know why it did; perhaps he didn't want to know.

The fact is, he had been having his meal in the hotel dining room when Lilian walked in, arm in arm with another man. With a word of apology to her companion, she immediately left him and made her way towards Roger as if she had expected, even planned to see him there.

"Hello handsome. How did the day in the park go with Cynthia? Exciting, I'll wager," she asked straight-faced.

The hint of irony in her words didn't take him by surprise this time; her being there did, not to mention the compliment. He tried not to let it show.

"I did have fun, thanks. If you'll allow me to return the flattery, you are looking as elegant as you did this morning."

"Yesterday you saw me dressed as a member of the police department; today as the elegant daughter of another police officer; it's possible that tomorrow you'll see me dressed in a completely different fashion. Our mutual thinker friend would no doubt tell you that change is the only constant, so be ready to be surprised."

That turned out to be the end of their short meeting, except for the wickedly sensual smile that she turned and threw him as she was making her way to the bar and the gentleman awaiting her. Both then vanished, leaving him with the feeling of unease that persisted as he sat in the hotel armchair with his diary and broken pencil in his hands.

He promptly set out for the zoo and the hope of some tranquility. On his way to the bus stop near the busy quay and the café he inevitably bumped into Jack, red-faced and jovial. With the unsettling image of Lilian still fresh in his mind, Roger wasn't feeling up to a talk with her father; just in case.

"Don't you ever have a day off from policing?"

"And I'm glad to see you, too, Roger. Anyhow, I see you've gotten up this morning on the other foot. We all have bad days. I also see that you've changed your look; jeans, T-shirt and soft shoes. You look even younger than yesterday, although there's no hiding a troubled expression, is there?"

Jack had to suffice with a courteous smile and a quick recital as to Roger's hurry to get where he was going. So, with a sigh of relief that was kept skillfully hidden from Jack's sight —or so he wished- the youthfully dressed financier ran to catch the bus that had been conveniently held up by an old lady who had to be helped aboard. He looked out of the glass protector and gave a timid wave to the somewhat bewildered figure who hadn't yet taken his eyes off of the receding friend who was now kicking himself for his foolish behavior; why shouldn't he tell Jack about the short conversation with his daughter? Then again, he consoled himself, something told him that he had done the right thing in keeping his silence.

The bus went past the woodland stop where he and Cynthia had alighted the day before, and the zoo was soon approaching. The aspect it gave was not the most appealing. In truth, it looked rather squalid, an evaluation that was soon confirmed when he paid his entrance fee and began his walk around. The Head of Maintenance of the gardens on the other side of the fence was right about the zoo being slowly run down with a view to finally closing it once and for all.

There was an exception to the ruling that Cynthia hadn't told him about; most likely because it was no more than a proposal that had been left unfinished and would, in all probability, come to nothing. He found out about it for himself when he came across the huge space that had been set aside and worked on, but that was now abandoned to its luck.

He searched for an attendant and after a while was able to put the question to a green booted worker, who told him that he was in the right: the site was supposed to have been the place in which the gorillas could live out their placid lives.

At the mention of the powerful yet gentle animal, Roger's eyes were transformed into two brightly lit saucers. He hardly took in the rest of the amiable zoo keeper's clarification about the one-time project: namely that the zoo was to be closed and the animals transferred to other installations. All except the gorillas, who were to live and hopefully breed in a large area that tried to recreate their native jungles. The animals wouldn't be as plainly visible as they are when behind bars, rather they would have to be observed from behind glass barriers that simulated the tropical vegetation.

"In that way, we could still have enjoyed seeing them while helping them in their fight against extinction. It's a pity the money ran out when the late Mayor passed away and his deputy took over the City Council. Just got the news this morning, as it goes. This new Mayor is certainly in a hurry to see the end of the place. No letting it slowly fade into the past."

"So they'll be shipped from here to another zoo?"

"Sooner or later, I'm afraid, along with the other animals. In the meantime, I'll keep feeding them the same as ever. Bye."

"Hold on. It's your job to feed the gorillas?"

"You caught me on my way there."

"Would you mind if I came along?" he almost begged.

Oliver, as the keeper's name turned out to be, had no objections whatsoever to having company. If Roger was the timid sort, he was a social creature, which meant that his jaw never stopped wagging. To Roger's delight, he began to furnish his newly found companion with what he wanted to know about the primates that had fascinated him ever since he first saw them as a child. In his hometown, he had lived a long way away from the zoo, a distance he sometimes covered on foot with some friends. Once there, though, they had to sneak inside by means of lifting the fence and sliding under, none of them ever having any money. In today's politically correct language they would be said to have been of humble origins; back then they were just poor. Roger never gave it a thought, of course. To him they were neither well nor badly off; they were simply a handful of adventurers having the time of their lives.

The two men arrived in a question of minutes, the caretaker pulling out the sacks of food from a shed for which he had the key, while still chattering away to his guest.

"I see that you are almost as fond of these beasts as I am," he said to a breath-taken Roger who had taken sight of the great leader and protector of the troop: the silverback. He soon recovered his composure, while completing his knowledge of how they lived.

"What's inside the sacks? What do they eat? Can I lend a hand?" he asked with bubbling enthusiasm.

"Of course, you can," responded Oliver pleasantly while pointing out more provisions stacked in a corner. "You can't go inside with the animals because they don't know you, but you can help me carry those boxes to the entrance gate. My back you know. The years can't be fooled. Anyway, no use complaining, is there?"

Roger wouldn't have made a fuss even if he had been told that the boxes that the keeper had indicated had been full of rocks. They were in fact enclosing a load of fruits, as he was told forthwith: these were lowland gorillas, and for the main part survived on the contents of what the trainee feeder was carrying, along with the plants that the long serving man in charge was stoutly dragging. The effort didn´t seem to affect his ability for talking, however.

"Vegetarians, you might say. Not as strict as the human variety, I must admit; those guys in there also eat insects. Mostly ants, but they´re one of God´s creatures too, I say."

Roger could find no flaw in Oliver´s point of view. He had no choice but to conclude that the supposedly less intelligent of the two species was also less incoherent - and maybe less extremist.

He let the human dilemma fade quickly from his mind and got back to more important things. His perpetually chattering friend was saying that from the entrance, he could observe the interaction between the members of the group and their well-known feeder. Did they also consider him their friend? he asked himself, while sitting obediently by the gate.

The sun, too shy that day to show her still paltry face, walked the skies unseen by neither the human eyes that were observing the gorillas, nor by those of the great apes who were being observed by their unmoving close cousin. Not that it interested the gazer. He couldn´t have cared less about the clouds that were hiding the sun;

about the wind that was pushing the clouds; about the clouds that left their usual springtime gift in the form of two or three showers; about the resulting chill, the soggy clothes stuck to his skin, or the generally unkempt look that he showed to the passers-by. It was something that seemed to be coming a habit, he ruefully told himself.

Neither was he aware of being the object of observation. The unnoticed watcher came, stayed for a while, and then promptly went thoughtfully about her business. It may have been no more than a coincidence, but the spellbound financier had wondered, at one stage during his vigil, if he was being scrutinized. Not by some*one*, however, but by the imprisoned animals; were they aware of him sitting there for so many hours? If they were, they certainly made a good job of faking it.

In any case, and much to his disappointment, the time soon came for the public to abandon the zoo without him being able to ask Oliver about it. The attendant hadn´t shown up since the midday feed. So, he turned his eyes away from the enclosure towards the magnificent scenery of the park, considering the possibility of asking the high-minded and green-fingered Cynthia to help him resolve his doubts. He couldn´t see her and asked himself why she hadn´t made an appearance, as she said she might the day before. In the end, it was none of his business, he concluded, as he set his feet in the direction of the exit.

As he sat on the bench at the bus stop peering through the oncoming twilight for signs of the bus, he decided that he would seek her out the next morning, bright and early once again. Right now, his only desire was to get back to a shower, a meal, his diary and a sharpened pencil with which today's exciting events would be eagerly recorded.

That, at least, had been his plan, because almost as soon as he arrived at his temporary accommodation, and before he could begin to get out of his damp clothing, there was a knock at the door. The booming sound fooled him into thinking that there must be a strong masculine hand responsible for it, so that his face took on a look of amazement on opening to the person responsible. Contrary to what might have been expected under other circumstances, it was difficult to say if his facial expression was one of good fortune, or misfortune; he was at a loss as to what to think.

"May I come in, Roger? I'd like to chat with you about something very important."

The trader stiffened a little at the apparently concerned tone of Lilian's voice. Was it possible that she had come looking for him because she was in some kind of trouble? Or perhaps something had happened to Jack.

"Of course, come in. What's wrong?"

"Nothing is wrong with me; you look terrible, though. Another crazy day with Cynthia and her flowerbeds? You'd better be careful. She's so...delightful. When it suits her, she'll give you what you ask, but bear in mind that she'll never offer you what I can. Anyway, before I get down to business, do you mind if I take my overcoat off? It's hot in here. And why don't you fix us both a drink. Champagne would be nice."

The still bedraggled financier agreed wholeheartedly about the drink, so that while trying to come to grips with Lilian's bizarre allusions, he opened the cooler and took out one of the two bottles that were stored ready for use.

His guest, meanwhile, had rid herself of the heavy black Mack that she usually wore when on duty in today's weather. Roger turned to offer the glass of sparkling wine and ask about the reason for her visit - now that it was obvious about there being no motive for distress - but the words were unable to take form: the police officer was dressed in a black skintight, one-piece dress that ended just above her knees. The rest of the way down was all black silk and matching high-heeled shoes. Had she just clarified the surprising comparison between herself and Cynthia made a few seconds ago? he asked in silence.

"I told you that you would see me dressed differently today, didn't I? I'm glad to see that it meets with your approval."

He couldn't refute the statement - or understatement; but neither could he allow himself to succumb to her designs as if he were a naive teenager.

"Listen, now that you've taken the trouble to get dressed up, why not let me offer you somewhere to go? I've spent most of the day alone and I fancy a pleasant talk over a tasty meal; we can get to know one another a little. You drink up while I get dressed and call a taxi."

He decided on a restaurant that purported to offer its clients a comfortably intimate atmosphere, according to the publicity he found lying on the dressing table.

On arrival, they spoke as any couple might do on a first date; of this and that, nothing too profound. What was missing, Roger noted, was the intense interest shown, or the nervous laughter that was usually provoked by whatever the other said, however banal or lacking in humor it might be. Unlike his first candid conversation with Cynthia, they both seemed to be wary of not showing either their true identity, nor their idiosyncrasies, secret wishes, hopes and fears.

In particular, the exotically perfumed woman before him never at any time strayed outside her attitude of impassive cynicism, albeit wrapped in a sensual coating. It wasn't that he judged her negatively; on the contrary, he believed her to be using both characteristics on show this evening as a shield against revealing herself; not only to him, but to the world in general. She kept something below the superficial façade that he sensed to be some kind of grudge against some sort of imaginary foe – even he found it hard not to feel guilty.

Nonetheless, as he continued observing her ever more closely, he became acutely aware of being over simplistic in his analysis, and so of the possibility of falling into the trap of stereotyping her.

After a time – and a couple of glasses of champagne – he even began to recriminate himself for being the cold, calculating observer. "You're not here assessing a future client, idiot," he said silently, "you're on holiday, having a drink with a beautiful, sexy woman. Relax and enjoy the experience."

He did as he was told and the change in his own disposition was automatically met with a reciprocal shift in Lilian's. Whether it was consciously done or no, he couldn't say – in fact, he followed his self-given orders and didn't even ask. For the rest of the night, the two took on the appearance of being a perfectly normal couple. So much so that towards the end of it Roger was letting loose typically corny set phrases.

"So, tell me, officer, why is it that you haven't settled down and had some children?"

"Because I haven't found the right father for them – nor the right husband for me."

"Well answered, Miss…?"

"Ortega. It's Spanish, naturally, but I don't want to go into the details of why I use my mother's surname, nor even talk about her, if you don't mind."

"Fine with me. Well then, Lilian Ortega, let me call you a cab. You can't walk home alone so late at night."

"Are you trying to get rid of me so quickly, then?"

"Not at all. I've enjoyed our first date, but I'm sure we both have to be up early tomorrow. Besides, I hope there will be other occasions to get to know one another a little more. Thanks for a wonderful evening – and I hope I didn't overly bore you with my talk on gorillas."

"Of course not. I've enjoyed our first date enormously too," she replied, mimicking his phrase in a tone that carried a mixture of mockery. The abrupt end to the evening had obviously brought out the bitter side of her personality once again.

"By the way," she said as the taxi door closed behind her, "don't forget, we have to talk about something important, but as you are in such a hurry to get to sleep, it'll have to be left for tomorrow. Sweet dreams."

Chapter Six

The open windows allowed the salt laden wind to blow both the curtains and Roger's hair at will. Unfortunately, his morning ritual was interrupted time and again by the memory of the night before. It was true that the misgivings he had harbored about the beautiful policewoman had been dispelled almost in their entirety; yet for some reason he had hardly been able to sleep.

To Roger's credit, he took the bus, walked along the woodland track, entered exactly as he had done as a kid (under the fence), and was there in the park early, just as he had planned the evening before. His lack of sleep was portrayed for all to see by the way he trudged along the neatly trimmed lawns in search of the buildings that served as shelter for the tropical plants - and Cynthia's office.

He had just turned the corner of the farthest of the greenhouses when his eye was caught by a familiar figure coming out from a large group of rhododendrons by way of a path that was man-made, but clearly overgrown and abandoned – well, almost. Roger quickly stepped back to where he couldn't be seen. Another mystery to be solved, he thought, but one that would have to be left for a better moment. He wasn't one for mysteries, but these last couple of days had been nothing more than the discovering of strange events – and people.

Then again, maybe he was being melodramatic, he thought to himself; his new acquaintances were just people like himself, each with their personal stories to tell and to be listened to. Even he had felt the need to do so and found benefit from it. Not, for certain, the type of benefits that he was accustomed to accumulate in his years as a broker. No, something that he was starting to see as much more valuable: the sharing of the grief, the pain, the deceptions, as well as the joys of our everyday lives.

He stooped to look at some flowers that were growing by the greenhouse, so that when Cynthia turned the corner, she found him there as if it were a surprise for both of them.

"Roger!" she said, "you´ve arrived at my favorite time of the day, when you can still see the dew on the plant life, when everything is so alive, so exuberant; waiting expectantly for the unfolding of the new day."

"Now you sound like a philosopher, Cynthia. I do suppose that you are extending the idea to the likes of you and me, as well as the unconscious forms of life that now take up your time. What I mean to say, in a roundabout way, is that I wholeheartedly agree; there´s nothing like the early morning, is there?"

"So, are you an early bird like me?" the gardener asked keenly. "Judging from your face, though, you enjoyed a late night as well. Am I wrong?"

"It's not what you think; with so much happening, I found it difficult to sleep, that's all. Is it so noticeable?"

"Not at all, it's just an intuitive guess," she answered in an ironic tone.

The bleary-eyed investor would have liked to have had a chat about the visitor he guessed was being alluded to and who had been responsible for his tossing and turning but desisted. In the first place, he wasn't sure he was in the right; how could Cynthia have possibly known? Secondly, it would be totally improper for him to do so with someone who had shown signs of hostility towards her, not to mention Lilian's more than corresponding feelings. A wide birth of the subject was the wisest course to take.

"In any case," he went on jovially, "do you know what I did yesterday? I visited the zoo, got to know the keeper, and he let me help him with the food for the gorillas. I stayed there all day, just sitting and watching those fascinating creatures."

"I know. I was watching the watcher from afar."

"And you didn't come and say hello? I looked for you. I wanted to chat a while."

"Well, here you have me for whatever you desire."

It was an innocent comment, but it once again reminded Roger of the night before, of something that Lilian had said about Cynthia in her inimitably habitual style – to put it lightly.

"You look troubled," the lady in question said, "why don't you accompany me while I go about my labours - my artistry - and tell me what it is that's on your mind."

The financial whiz thought about making recourse of his encounter with the gorillas so as not talk about what had provoked the anguished face that so obviously gave his feelings away. It was a way out, but one that only made him feel guilty about not being sincere to his new friends: here he was, supposedly starting a new life, looking to recover the happiness that he had savoured as a child while doing something that had little to do with his endeavours. Namely, behaving in a deceitful way. He recognized the truth of his own internal deliberation, and bravely corrected his conduct.

"It's about last night; the late night, as you rightly said."

He paused a second to gain momentum; this was damned hard going. "Lilian paid me a visit in my hotel room. She asked me for a drink, so I took her to a restaurant where we shared a bottle of champagne together."

"Then you shared other things that we won't mention?" Cynthia said with her usual calm. "Before you continue, let me say that I appreciate your confidence in me. It's not always easy to come out with the 'naked truth', shall we say."

Roger was staggered; he had hardly expected such a candid, although erroneous, comment. His principal worry had been her possibly adverse reaction, but as it happened, she didn't seem to be in the slightest put out; she had even joked about it. Maybe he had been silly to have harboured such thoughts.

"Anyway," the philosopher carried on, "why the troubled expression? *Did* something *untoward* happen that you can't tell me about?"

"Nothing substantial, as I said before – certainly not along the lines you are tracing with your, let's say, vivid imagination. I can't give you anything concrete on what she said or did, it's simply an uncomfortable feeling that I have. All we did was to go out for a drink, over which she even turned out to be quite charming at times, but I feel now that I've gone and done something I shouldn't have; something that will only complicate my visit here and that might possibly affect my relationship with Jack – and with you."

Now it was Cynthia's turn to be taken at unawares, although she gave no sign of it being so.

"I'm all ears?" she asked succinctly.

"The thing that bothers me most is that I didn't come here to get caught up in a torrid affair."

"Torrid?" she asked softly. "Why do you use that precise word? Surely it was only two people having drink together, or so you said. Aren't you being a touch melodramatic about it all? Then again, maybe it's me who's jumping the gun. I should let you fill in the details before making assumptions. Please, carry on."

"Well, from the little I've seen, Lilian would appear to have a 'convulsed' personality. She reminds me of the sea; unpredictable and uncontrollable - and you know my aversion to the dark depths. In any case, you should have more knowledge about her than I do. No?"

"Our opinions about her coincide, if that's what you mean. The only thing I can say, however, is that if you feel the way you do, you only have to tell her what you've told me; that, at least for the moment, you are quite happy alone and... unencumbered. Then get on with what you came here to do."

"I thought that you philosophers were given to complexities and abstractions when evaluating what goes on in the world. Isn't your solution ever so slightly simplistic? I mean, putting it into practice might not be as straightforward as you propose."

"You forget that I'm now a gardener. My 'philosophy', as you put it, is no longer an airy-fairy, pie in the sky, ivory tower type. That's exactly why I left the clouds to soil my hands," she remarked, smiling serenely at the memory of Roger's poetic remark on hearing about her past life on that first day together here in the park. "I assure you that my words are based on experience, or close observation. I wouldn't ask you to do something that I wouldn't do - or haven't already done."

Roger, smiling in his turn at her subtle humor, knew that she was referring to her own personal relationship with the detective who had asked for her aid in trying to resolve the mysterious crime that Cynthia had told him about. Despite his plea for advice, she decided not to elaborate on how things had gone between them, on the chain of events that had led to her having an opinion of Lilian similar to the one that Roger was forming, albeit against his will; he had seen momentary glimpses of someone sweet and tender, even innocently enthralling.

Strangely enough, Cynthia was lamenting the fact that there were many details which couldn't be told, it not being for her to compromise someone by filling other's minds with preconceptions about them; even Jack, for whom she felt a deep affection, couldn't know from her mouth some of her thoughts about his daughter, in spite of the reserves she had on holding back. This naturally produced a moral conflict; shouldn't she be as forthcoming with both men as Roger had been with her?

She gave a sigh. "Do you think I should stop being so discreet and, rather, come out and speak my mind?"

"Are you asking *me* for advice?" he replied, "or are you falling back into your old Platonic dialogues when discussing what took place between you and Lilian? That's to say, between Lilian and yourself?"

"You are hilarious, aren't you?" she said straight-faced, after which she went on to say that nobody -not even she- had the copyright to the truth; at most their own truth, which they can only exchange with everyone else. Although we are all unique, one person's experiences can serve as a guide for others to find their way. Of course, it would be a path that had for each a different course - but not for that should it be rejected out of hand. With one exception: anything imposed, or anyone claiming to know what is best for the rest of us must *never* be listened to.

The speaker's last emphatic assertion made her listener's mind go hurtling back to the time when he, at the age of ten or so, had been part of a small religious group who met in an apartment to praise the divinity that held their belief system in its hands. Or rather, now that he thought about it after all these years, he recognized that it wasn't so. Maybe the deity existed, maybe not, but who controlled their wills in his case was the preacher, someone who had rejected official church doctrine, had rounded up his own little flock and was leading them where he would. Some of his followers even lived in the flat, sheepishly handing in their wages – every last penny, as part of "living the true experience", the way it had been commanded to be – at least according to the minister.

Despite the recollection of being, in his innocence, as happy as a lark at the time, the memory that now struck him most was of the prohibitions; there always seemed to be so many. Luckily for him, his family had had to move home, so he had been inadvertently taken away from someone who - just as Cynthia had said – imposed his supposed knowledge of what he and the rest of the group should or shouldn´t do to achieve the compassion of whom they were all worshipping.

Roger came back from the past and gave his attention once again to the thought-provoking woman who was staring into his eyes, awaiting his return. He knew that apart from her reticence to give her opinion on Lilian, she was now extrapolating from the strictly personal circumstances they had been discussing to a criticism of world affairs in general, especially the politicians and those who wielded power and influence over the inhabitants of the planet. He felt he saw an inconsistency in her speech – and he didn´t hesitate in taking the liberty of letting her know of his deliberations.

"If that´s your point of view, why don´t you try to change things instead of building a refuge here amongst the trees and flowers? If you care about the injustices that exist in the world, why don't you find a pedestal and proclaim those well-founded views?"

"There you go passing sentence again," she said with a hint of irritation. "Do I judge you for the things you do?"

"So why did you just tell me what I should or shouldn't do with my life?"

"I like to break my own rules now and again," she ended with a mischievous smile that, despite her doubts about unduly giving personal opinions, smacked of both self-confidence as well as self-indulgence.

Roger shivered. On this occasion, though, it wasn't a consequence of the conversation – which had reached a stalemate - but of the brisk chill that the inward-rolling mists had brought with no forewarning. It was a cold salty moisture that found no defenses to overcome in their endeavor to penetrate right to the broker's bones: he hadn't brought an overcoat.

What heightened the effect was the tree-lined tunnel that they found themselves in as they were now walking along what had once been a railway track, Cynthia explained, and that was now used by the visitors to the park to go from what was the main part of the gardens to another smaller area, not so immaculately cared for, but still as charming – as Roger would soon find out.

They stepped out of the mile-long path into the open space. On the left was a small picnic area –empty as yet-with the typically wooden tables and benches that gave the users a spectacular view: the right-hand side of where they had left the tunnel soon ended in a cliff, from where they could look out over the seaside town and then on out to ocean itself. The fog didn't allow them to see anything very clearly right at that moment, but Roger could imagine the beauty of the sight on a clear summer morning.

Just as had happened in the ice-cream parlour a few days ago, and again in his hotel room, he was overwhelmed by the memories of times past. Or rather, he was *almost, but not quite,* overcome: the delightful sensation he felt began making its decline when it reached a certain point in the metaphorical distance; elusively close, annoyingly elusive, like a comforting sound in the distance that can't be pinpointed and that finally ends by fading disappointingly away. There was something missing, some… thing he couldn't even name that would always be out of reach. Yes, he mused sullenly, he felt at a loss as to what to think, what to do and where to go.

"You're on another one of your trips down memory lane, I suppose," Cynthia said amiably. "And now the morning doesn't seem so vivacious. You know you have to get back to living the present, however it may present itself. That's where the answer is hiding, not in the past."

"Yes," Roger replied with a forced laugh. "The happiness that these flash-backs bring never fully materializes. It's quite frustrating."

"Don't let it get you down. These feelings never will take hold of you like they did for the boy you were. For him they were real. You have to be happy living out new realities in the here and now, too."

"Two days ago, I asked you how, and you were… 'reluctant' to give the secret away."

"There is no secret, Roger."

The young broker looked towards the skies, almost frenzied by the habit she had of never giving a concrete answer. Cynthia put her hand on his shoulder.

"Now don't sulk, Roger, and don't get anxious, because if you do it's a sure thing that you won't ever be able to calmly spread your wings and soar on the warm winds of happiness."

"Has no-one ever told you that your nuts?"

"Believe it or not, I 'm glad to say that you are the first to do so. My only response is to say that being a little crazy is what keeps me sane."

Roger laughed an authentic laugh at her clever humor. In fact, he found it more than just comical, it was very enticing.

"That's quite a whimsical paradox," he affirmed unnecessarily, "is it one of your own vintage?

"Yes. And made up on the spur of the moment, to boot," she said with mock pride. "Which just happens to remind me about the 'secret', as you put it."

"Well, at last. The day as yet promises."

"As I see it," she went on with a nod of appreciation for the confidence he showed her, "you've lived out a fifteen-year plan, true? Now it's time for a return to spontaneity! Go where your heart invites you to go without your calculator in hand. Needless to say, you'll make mistakes; you know that yourself. But it's part of the adventure, isn't it? One more piece of advice: don't ever desire happiness as if it were a craving for riches, or power, or even a woman; that will surely frighten it away."

"Now you begin to sound like a someone offering a beautiful gift, but with a kindly warning attached," he said. Then he looked straight into her eyes, menacing her with a look of Shakespearean solemnity. "Do you know what the most threatening thing about acting on a whim is?"

"No," answered Cynthia, while trying not to laugh at his play-acting. "Tell me about it."

Roger saw that her astuteness was not to be easily overcome. So, he shrugged his shoulder and went back to being himself again.

"It leaves you hungry," he said with a grin. "I only came running here to chat with you at dawn and forgot about breakfast, didn´t I?"

"You see? Your bravery will be rewarded. Back in my little office by the greenhouses I have all the necessaries to beat off the hunger."

Roger was soon marveling to find that it was indeed as the Lighthouse of Alexandria (as he would one day describe Cynthia in his diary) had said. A mini apartment equipped with a cooking stove, a table, chairs, cutlery and a fridge replete with supplies. It was almost as if she lived there.

Did she? he suddenly asked himself as his eyes took in the dishes on the draining board, cleaned yesterday no doubt. Then he saw the bed-settee, flanked on either side by book-filled shelves.

She *is* living here! He felt sure about it. First, he recalled how they had come here together the other day, but he had gone home while she had made some excuse about having to stay to give orders to her staff; next, she had admitted to being here yesterday, but wasn´t on the last bus back to town after closing time; and finally, this morning he had arrived before the park was open and there she had been, coming through another private gate that probably led to more parklands. He would most certainly investigate that later, he reminded himself.

And yet, despite the austerity of the little place, she appeared as serene and carefree as anyone. Well, he corrected himself, as few people were able! Could he become one of those?

He watched her as she went about preparing the food that would break his fast; tea, of course (which he had the pleasure to prepare), but that would be served alongside a continental style array of victuals. While he waited for the kettle to boil, he began to have doubts: maybe he was jumping to unfounded conclusions, or it might be that his imagination had leapt and bounded beyond their usual confines. No, he finally concluded, there was certainly something deeper going on here that evaded his five senses – which was only natural, dealing as he was with a philosopher come gardener.

Although his curiosity about Cynthia was now rising exponentially, the pondering was soon put to an end. "Thanks," he said as he took the plate handed to him.

They sat and ate in silence, then sipped the hot tea while looking out of the small window onto the lawns that were now turning a lighter shade of green as the mists were slowly burned away by the climbing mid-spring sun.

The money-maker was itching to ask more questions, in particular about the police enquiry that Cynthia had mentioned on their first walk together. Intuition told him that, apart from the mystery of the case in itself, it was somehow entwined with what was going on between the two ladies who had entered his life. He looked at her pretty face and decided against the idea, so engrossed in other things as she appeared to be.

So, with the bare minimum of words they split up for the rest of the day. Cynthia thoughtfully attending the blossoming flora while Roger set about his investigations – once he had paid the obligatory visit to the gorillas and helped Oliver with their feed. In the end, he had to drag himself away with a sigh full of regret; his role as private investigator had to be got underway. Well, he'd be back tomorrow, he promised the creatures.

It was still only mid-afternoon when Roger took an outside seat at the café in front of the fishing port. He was equipped with the laptop computer that he had hidden away under his hotel bed with the idea of only using in the case of an emergency, which he now thought to be the case. He felt it urgent to know a few things about the two women who had made his life, if not topsy-turvy, at least interesting.

The first thing to do was to go into the internet maps and see just what there was beyond the hidden private gate discovered this morning. From where had Cynthia made her unexpected appearance? He found the park with the zoo, pulled the screen over to the area he was interested in, and zoomed in as far as it was permitted.

He was fascinated to find that the path led to what looked like another huge and well-tended area of parkland, similar to the one he had come to know, except that in what was more or less the centre there was a fairly small sized stately mansion.

He made note of the name of the estate and searched for details in the web. The owner of Longstone House, as it was called, was a member of the nobility, one Lady Waverley. Roger promptly logged out of the website and began rubbing his stubbly chin.

Fancy that, he thought to himself, Cynthia is looking after two places at the same time: one belonging to aristocracy and the other owned by the local government. No wonder she has to live in the small office/apartment at the back of the greenhouses; she can´t have time for travelling to and from town. He was filled with admiration at her capacity, yet surprised that she should have chosen such a hard life when she could have been living comfortably in the world of academia. He would ask her about it the next day – maybe this time he would receive an answer.

Now it was time to look for something on Lilian. Being a detective, he suspected that he wouldn´t get far – and he was right. Apart from the restricted information, the only mention he found on her were newspaper reports on the murder case that the hard-working Cynthia had lent a hand in. The case had, effectively, finished unresolved, just as she had told him, yet what was really interesting about the investigation was the fact that the victim was the former town mayor!

After re-reading the information, it suddenly struck him that there was no mention of the gardener, or the exotic flower that she had identified. He scratched his chin once again; it was all very peculiar.

Yet another perplexing thought came to his mind; neither of the two woman involved in the case, and now in his life, had spoken clearly about what must surely have been one of the biggest events to have taken place in the small town for the last years. Another unexplained silence that added to his already perplexed state of mind.

"Why the secrecy in the newspaper?" he sighed, feeling himself suddenly estranged, at once oppressed and exhilarated by the accumulation of events. One thing was for certain, he now had more enigmas for his growing file.

All of a sudden, his computer advised him of an incoming e-mail. He had hidden the thing away under his bed, as well as leaving his mobile phone at home, because he had wanted to totally disconnect from his former life for a while. But there was no harm in seeing who the sender might be, he told himself; after all, there was no need to answer, was there?

"What the hell……" he blurted out load, receiving in the process not a few strange looks from the other customers sitting nearby.

He opened and read the message. He was expected at eight o´clock that evening in the hotel lounge, where he would be picked up and driven to an important event at the town hall. Lilian added, either rashly or ironically, that he would be glad to hear that she would form part of the reception committee, indeed he would be her escort for the night. Either way, he was in no way pleased with the message.

"But how did she get my address?" asked an angry Roger, the answer jumping immediately at him: the only possible way was for her to have made use of her police contacts!

"The woman isn´t averse to stooping to Big Brother tactics. She´s broken the laws of privacy just to get in contact with me. What kind of a woman is she? And how did she know I had my computer with me?" he said under his voice while looking suspiciously from side to side. "And I´ve no intention of going anywhere tonight, either with or without you," he finished out loud as if he thought she could hear him.

His look of indignation turned to one of desperation when he detected a blue uniformed figure sauntering along against the background of the sparkling darkness of the ocean – he was in no mood for a chat.

Fortunately, the silhouette appeared to be impervious, as yet, of Roger's presence in the café, so that he bent as close to the computer screen as he could, hoping against hope that it would shield him from the policeman's sight; and therefore, form a most uncomfortable meeting.

Jack began to dwindle as he continued along the sea front, but that only meant that Roger's worries over tonight's events began to grow. He hurriedly collected his things from the small table and made his way back to the hotel.

Chapter Seven

As Roger would promptly write in his outlandish diary, he was punctually sitting in the hotel lounge when a familiar figure made his not unexpected appearance. As it turned out, he had reluctantly answered Lilian´s e-mail, saying that he had no intention of dining with the mayor, and less so of being presented as the new man in her life. On that matter, he said that they had to get together - and talk clearly.

Her reply was most apologetic: she was in no way going to insinuate such a thing; the dinner would be strictly business, and quite formal. There would also be a surprise announcement by the mayor who would be accompanied by the top members of the police department and local government officials. She also mentioned that the man who Roger had just seen entering the hotel and who was now making his way smartly towards him would also be attending, from which he guessed that he would most likely be the focus of attention.

For that reason, and that reason alone – he desperately tried to convince himself - he acquiesced. Lilian had also alluded in her message to Roger´s presence being solicited by the politician, but as nothing was made clear it didn't affect his decision one way or the other and that was that. He stood up to offer his greetings.

"Hello Jack, pleased to see you again. I'm glad you're coming along, because I don't see what I'm supposed to be doing there amongst politicians and police chiefs. Lilian said something about me talking financial affairs with the mayor, but I'm sure I don't have the slightest idea of what she might be referring to."

"Maybe he wants to invest in the stock-exchange. If that's the case, then you are the best man for the job, I believe you said."

"Of course, that must be it. Why didn't it occur to me?" Roger replied, astutely concealing his lack of conviction; he had certainly thought of that possibility but had a suspicion that it was going to be about something completely different from his friend's logical deduction. He was convinced that recent events endorsed his hypothesis. "Anyway," he continued, "I've been told that there will be some sort of official ceremony taking place. Do you know anything about it?"

"Only that it involves my daughter, and that the press will be there along with all the town big-wigs. Just what it concerns is a mystery to me. Although I do have my speculations – which might be nothing more than hopes, if you catch my drift. Why else would I be invited if not," he finished tentatively.

"I see you're not willing to tell me what you expect. So much the better; it'll be a surprise for both of us."

Lilian was there in person to take them into the dining room when they arrived. She showed them to their designated tables after a peck on the cheek for her father and a handshake for Roger, who found it no surprise to see her elegantly, but discretely dressed in a fashion that Jack would approve of.

Their table was next to that of the mayor, who came round during the meal to introduce himself. He had met Jack on previous occasions, and so greeted him warmly; he also somehow knew who it was that accompanied the sergeant without the need for introductions. Roger also recognized the politicians face: he was the stranger who had been with Lilian when they accidently bumped into each other in the hotel bar– if that was what you could call it. A brief handshake and a concise "Mr. Penrose, I'm so pleased to meet you. We must have a chat later, if you would be so kind", and he was gone again as if he were fishing for votes.

He looked for Lilian's whereabouts only to find her eyes fixed on him, before turning quickly away to talk with the mayor's wife; she had been invited to sit in a place of distinction between the two. Somehow things began to look suspiciously sordid, which once again modified his opinion of the detective, in line with the negative trend of before.

He turned his face and his thoughts to her father. "Well then, Jack, let's enjoy the rest of the dinner while we wait for events to unfold. Tell me about you and your family."

The on-the-beat police sergeant began by explaining that his wife had left him some twenty years ago and that he had never entered into any kind of stable, or lasting relationship since then. Amidst Roger's words of regret, he then told of the love and pride he felt for his only daughter, not to mention the sense of pity that he sometimes felt for the breaking of the ties with her mother. It appeared that her feelings for her father were as strong as his own towards her; so much so that Lilian had neither forgiven, nor made contact with her mother, in spite of the fact that they all lived in a small community where avoiding anyone for a length of time was a feat in itself.

Roger was then surprised when his friend ventured to further explain that Lilian's unstable lifestyle had been reflected in various short-lived affairs with what he deemed to be 'undesirables' and that he desperately hoped she would soon meet someone who would give her the love she needed to receive -and to give. "Deep down she has a noble, tender heart, and life is about sharing. Don't you think?"

Roger whole-heatedly agreed, even though he himself hadn't faired any better in his romances than Lilian had. Yet what struck him was the idea that Jack should be telling him about his daughter's emotional mishaps; to what end?"

He preferred not to enquire any further, already making the obvious guess. Namely, that he might be the 'Mr. Right' she was looking for. As much as he was flattered by Jack's positive opinion about himself, he avoided the issue by going back to the mother.

"So, your ex -sorry, Lilian's mother- still lives in the town, then?" Roger asked, expressing his evident surprise.

"Oh, yes," Jack retorted quickly. "You see, she married the branch director of one of the big banks. I go past the place on my beat several times a day."

Roger imagined it to be tough on his friend to have to suffer something like that daily. His heartfelt pity was unexpectedly soothed, nevertheless, by the policeman's following phrase.

"That's one good thing about retirement, though; it means I won't ever be obliged to do so again." He laughed for the first time that evening while raising his glass in a gesture of celebration.

"Really?" Roger exclaimed, "you mentioned it the other day, but never said that it would be so immediate. Well, well, that makes us two retired, single, foot-loose and fancy-free young men."

"I don't know about 'young', Roger, but it doesn't sound at all bad, I'll give you that."

Just as they were about to consummate the toast, the mayor stood up and called for everyone's attention; he was about to make the awaited-for proclamation. The waiter's had cleared the tables and the local press were quickly gathering round. The surprise announcement turned out to be just what the broker suspected Jack to have suspected.

The politician began by giving a short speech on the merits of being a dutiful police officer, ending with a request for Jack to come forward; his years of service were going to be acknowledged by way of a 'small token of gratitude' on behalf of the town council and the police department in the form of an inscribed gold watch. It had ceased to be a custom nowadays, but the mayor clarified things by saying that this was a well-deserved exception.

Lilian, who -Roger was sure- had most certainly had a hand in bringing about the revival of the old tradition, was given the honor of handing over the gift to her father, after which she also gave him an emotional hug. He made his way, crimson faced, back to his seat beside Roger, who gave him a warm smile and a vigorous handshake.

Things weren't over yet, as it immediately became clear. Indeed, the real eye-opener was straightaway to be unveiled. The proud daughter had remained on her feet beside the mayor, which could only mean that as well as knowing about what had just taken place, she also knew what was coming next. Without any fuss or ceremony, it was announced that she was to be promoted to head of the police department.

Roger looked into her beaming father's flabbergasted eyes, now awash with tears that went unnoticed by the rest of the dispersing crowd. "Shall we congratulate the new chief of police, then?" he said heartily. Whatever else might be going on, he sincerely felt delighted for them both and demonstrated it by giving her a passionate hug. He finally stepped back, surprised at the spontaneous show of emotion, yet also knowing that they had both shared the experience. Jack promptly, although unwittingly broke the scene up.

Things unexpected weren't at an end, however, because while Lilian received her father's felicitations, Roger found out the reason for his being invited. The head of the town council took him politely aside and, just as Jack had said, spoke about an investment that he was interested in, the nature of which, nonetheless, would leave the trader stunned, to put it mildly.

It had nothing at all to do with Roger's usual line of work. In fact, there was no money to be made at all.

"No," the mayor said in a matter-of fact voice, "it has to do with our little town. I take it you do like the place. You've spent time here as a child, I've been informed."

"That's correct. I suppose the new chief of police is the informer?" he replied with equal calm; the bombshell hadn't yet to be thrown at him, but it was on its way.

"In part, as is only natural," answered the politician. "Anyway Roger, I'll come straight to the point; don't you think that this would be a great location for settling down and raising a family?"

"I beg your pardon?" came the financier's choked remark.

The mayor carried on as if he were now in a hurry. "Hence the idea of an investment in your future. It just so happens that the zoo you seem to be so fond of is part of the Longstone Estate, the running of which has been ceded to the local government. Now imagine that you were to be the owner of the whole lot!"

"Me?" said Roger, now totally astounded at what he was hearing. "It just so happens I know a little about the place, but would you kindly explain just exactly what you are referring to?"

"Of course, my good fellow, of course. The fact of the matter is that the Longstone estate will be up for auction very soon. That's to say, the mansion, the lands, as well as the zoo. Which would be handed back to you for its management, if you desire. You see, the owner, Lady Waverley, is in debt to the banks *and* to the taxman. Her late father made some dubious purchases which haven't turned out beneficial for her. You could be her savior."

The mayor saw that the investor was taking interest in what he was feeding him, so he added another ingredient. "The thing is," he said, lowering his voice, "in an auction, you would be no more than one of many bidders, and we don't want the place taken over by some foreign billionaire with a sack full of petrodollars; no one in the town at any rate is overly enthusiastic about such a prospect. What's more, I doubt if you are in the position to compete with such types."

"So, what are you suggesting? Always supposing I'm in the market."

"It's like this, Roger. I have my contacts, you understand. I'm sure there's no need to go into details that you can probably guess. In any case, I'm acquainted with certain people who are willing to accept the cancelling of the debts in partial (as a personal favour to me, one might humbly say). Always, of course, to someone who can put sufficient money up front before the auction takes place officially, and who I consider might merit such... consideration."

Roger thought for a few seconds on the legal and moral implications. Despite his misgivings, the idea was enticing, not least the thought of holding in his hands the destiny of his cherished gorillas.

"Just out of curiosity, exactly how much money are we talking?" he asked in his calm and collected business style.

The politician took out a pen, scribbled a number on a napkin and gave him the figure as if he knew full well that it wasn't an amount that Roger couldn't afford.

"And the Lady? What does she think about it? What will happen to her?"

"She doesn't really have much say in the matter. Between you and I, you are her best option. I took the liberty of suggesting that in an auction there is always the risk that she might not get enough to even cover the debts. She has other properties which she would be forced to sell, or have confiscated."

What Roger heard sounded reasonable and fair; he didn't like the idea of an old lady living the twilight of her life in poverty. Even so, and whatever his final decision might be, he wanted to have a chat with the owner beforehand.

"Two things," he said, still businesslike in his manner. "I want some time to think it over, and I'd like to see the place as soon as you can arrange it. Tomorrow, if it's possible, although no doubt you'll have to get in touch with the Lady of the Manor."

"Said and done, my dear fellow, said and done. I'll even get someone to take you there. Have you picked up at ten o´clock, shall we say? In that way you´ll have the whole day to look it over. I´ll also expect your call in the evening," he finished handing his private card to Roger.

"A little more time than that, Charles," he said with a cold look of dissatisfaction look on his face. He didn´t like demands being made upon him, and he was in the fortunate position of not having to put up with them – ever again. The sudden realization of one of the more pleasant consequences of his fortuitous financial and career situation then brought a generous smile to his face.

"I´m going home tomorrow afternoon," he said with less harshness, "probably until the weekend. I´ll give you a call then, if that´s alright."

The politician agreed with the same haste as he had shown during the short, but intense conversation. Then they shook hands and parted, the mayor leaving by a back door, Roger taking the door through which he had entered. He found Jack and his daughter waiting patiently for the secret talk to come to an end, and soon all three were sitting in the back seats of the taxi that Jack had ordered.

After briefly explaining the mayor´s surprising ´offer´, Roger fell silent and took the role of observer. The first thing he noticed was Lilian´s change of mood. It was only natural, of course, given her promotion. What struck him, nevertheless, was that this was the first time he had seen the policewoman looking and sounding so lighthearted. The two were gently pulling one another's leg. Roger might even have admitted to finding her laughter exhilarating in its childlike, simple sincerity.

In fact, his heart began to race while the rational side of him was asking if this was indeed the real Lilian: or was it the sultry mocking type who had visited him two nights before; or the angry zoo hater of two days before that; or the silent, serious police officer on the night of their first drizzly meeting.

They reached the hotel before Roger could go any further with his deliberations – at least, for the present. He shook Jack's hand, quickly explaining his plan to visit the Waverley Estate after breakfast the following morning before catching the mid-day train; he wanted to attend to some things back home before deciding on whether to purchase the lands – or not. Jack expressed his desire to see him again if he wished to return, while Lilian gave him a look so desperately sweet that it was almost blackmail; it demanded, and received, a heart wrenching reaction in Roger hitherto unknown to him. It left him both bewildered and nervous.

The last glance they shared as Roger closed the car door told him that she had recognized what he felt, and that she was similarly confused. What he couldn't say was whether her bemusement was down to the feelings that he had inadvertently shown – or to her own unexpectedly corresponding feelings towards him.

Chapter Eight

The next morning did indeed carry on from where the night had left off: the customary blast of cold air followed by the cup of hot coffee. In between he had put on his best suit, open neck silk shirt (on this occasion he dispensed with the customary tie) and brightly polished shoes – today was a business day, so that he was dressed as he had always done when investing important sums of money. It was more of an aid than anything else as it focused his mind where it needed to be; smart outfit, smart decisions, that was Roger's motto.

As he walked along the sea front enjoying the warmth of the sun and it's sparkling reflection on the endlessly changing surface of the bleak waters, he admitted to himself that today was no doubt an exception There was a lot more than a simple financial deal to be dealt with, now that his long-term future was in play, and that was a variable he had never had to face before -as was the part of the equation that involved the feelings aroused by the new chief of police. He had only ever experienced anything remotely similar, but that was in the remote past, he wryly concluded.

Yes, Lilian, he continued musing, the restless soul who, judging by his reaction the night before, had made an impression on him which went deeper than the purely physical, but who also aroused an uneasy suspicion of darker things to be discovered; the woman who enticed him like no-one before, but who also provoked a sense of caution that he couldn't explain; and why deny it, a woman who he found so damned attractive, yet with a personality that was in some way afflicted -however strong willed she might be.

As his stroll came to an end – he had to be at the hotel at ten o'clock – his attention was caught by the sight of a pale-yellow colored E-Type Jaguar from the 1960's, or so he guessed. It was parked in the very entrance to the hotel, something which should have been accompanied by a ticket on the windscreen or a tow truck at work, but neither traffic warden nor police were anywhere to be seen.

And where was the impudent owner, he asked himself while walking round the immaculately maintained body of the vehicle and observing closely the beautifully kept beige interior. As anyone watching him could easily have deduced, he loved vintage cars. He did, in fact, have at home in his garage a Ford Mustang that had come out of the factory in 66, along with a Porsche Spider from the 50's.

All of a sudden, and much to his surprise, he saw that the keys had been left in the starter by someone who he judged to be either a fool or very self-assured. He couldn't resist the temptation and, completely forgetting his previous criticisms, was soon sitting at the wheel, itching to turn the keys and head out of town.

He was so absorbed in his imaginary drive that he jumped out of his skin when a voice whispered the most sensual of good mornings in his unsuspecting ear.

"Lilian, what a fright you've given me," he spurted.

"Do I frighten you, then? You do disappoint me."

Roger supposed that she had gotten up today and dressed herself in her costume of sarcasm. "You just startled me out of my daydreaming," he said playfully, determined upon not allowing her to dampen his bright start to the day. "I love this car. But tell me, why is it that everything you say seems to have a double meaning? And I'm not frightened of you, I'm intrigued."

"Only 'intrigued'? It might be a compliment for someone like Cynthia, but I don't find it overly exciting." She said it in the smoldering volcano tone of voice of the night in the hotel room, provoking Roger's annoyance. Before he could say what he thought, however, her shapely figure - topped by a headscarf and sunglasses that matched the era of the car - had moved elegantly around the front of the car, opened the door and put the seat belt on.

"What are you doing, exactly?" Roger asked straight-faced, even though he was impressed by the woman's cheek.

"Do I still intrigue you?" she laughed, apparently changing her disposition to one a little more affable. "You agreed to see the Longstone Estate, didn't you?

Well, I decided I'd take you personally on the tour; and in my own car."

"O… K…" he said enthusiastically, "So this is your little baby, is it? I take it you want me to drive?"

"That's exactly the way of it, darling. Take us home to the Manor so that we can forget for a while that the world exists and talk intimately, just you and I, about your clash with reality. Or do you by any chance believe that you can wipe clean away all the contamination you've accumulated over the years, the toxins that are responsible for your present predicament? I'm referring, of course, to your vain search for a lost idyllic childhood. Not to mention the girl who ran from you and your land of ice-cream and honey."

She sighed, half mocking, half playfully teasing. "And what does Cynthia think about it all, by the way?"

Roger decided not to turn the key as yet, but instead to respond to the unexpected provocation.

"Well, to my mind your description sounds a bit too radical, but yes, she did mention something about overcoming years of intoxication, if that's what you mean."

"Precisely. For example, one of the corrupting agents that poison our innocent young hearts is when we learn to lie, wouldn't you agree?"

"You are very erudite today, Lilian."

"For a simple detective, you mean to say? Do I surprise, as well as intrigue you?"

"You never fail to do either, Lilian. But getting back to our pleasant morning discussion; despite the accuracy of your treatise on our acquired experiences, I haven't lied and I'm not about to, either. Although I can't quite fathom what you're getting at, let me just say that the only crime I've committed is to allow myself to get carried away by my preconceived ideas of... certain people – for which I sincerely apologize. I might also add that my honesty is maybe the best way of refuting your, to my mind unjustified argument, wouldn't *you* agree? We live and learn, wouldn't you say?"

"Uhu," Lilian agreed with reserve, as she was undeterred and apparently willing to carry on, for some obscure and twisted reason, with her aim of destroying Roger's hopes of completing his quest. "What would say about our learning to feel pain – to inflict it on others. Tell me," she asked, sure of her victory, "how are we to dispel those shadows from our hearts, Roger?"

"By opening them?"

"And if you don't like what you see? Or hear? The strings of my heart only make the bitterest of sounds, as you've no doubt observed."

The investor, at once confused as to where the lady beside him was coming from and where she was going to with her unexpected words, decided to leave the absurd conversation aside and at last provoked the engine into life.

He drove with the same steady confidence with which he handled his business affairs while Lilian observed him out of the side of her eye. She liked the way he effortlessly controlled, even dominated, the car with such assuredness – she liked it a lot.

A halt was ordered to allow a couple to make use of the zebra crossing. Roger finally took his eyes off the road, looked into the pair of green eyes sparkling through the dark crystals and said simply, "You're talking nonsense."

Neither of the two uttered another word during what remained of the short journey; the driver giving his full concentration to the driving, while the passenger kept hers on the driver.

The car was brought skillfully to a halt at the main entrance to the house and Lilian jumped out with a sensation of exhilaration that she hadn't experienced in a long time. She outstretched her arms and yelled at the top of her voice, "Here I am at last. Let's check our new residence out!"

Roger, for as much as he might be feeling the excitement, was here on business – and that meant he never lost his nerve under any circumstances. He was thrilled to see that his guide had shrugged off her somber mood, but he also wondered about her talking about the mansion as if they were a couple looking to buy a home.

And yet despite his misgivings about her intentions, he felt something for her that was growing beyond the purely physical attraction and, although nothing had been said, he was sure that the feeling was mutual.

One thing was one thing, however, and another thing was something completely different, he joked with himself, remembering Cynthia's words on letting things take their course.

"So where is the Lady of the house, then?" he asked his beautiful hostess playfully. "She was advised of my coming, *wasn't she?*"

"Oh yes, of course she was," replied the woman dressed in a dazzling white trouser suit; she said it in an offhanded way that showed how mesmerized she was by the panorama, in spite of having visited the grounds during her investigation of the mayor's untimely demise.

The circumstances had changed, however, although she wasn't for a moment going to let Roger in on what was running through her mind. She turned to look at him with a seductive smile. "But you see, she's out of town for the day. She'll arrive back on the four o'clock train – or so I've been informed."

"I'm sorry to hear that," Roger responded in his best professional tone. "I'd have liked a chat with the old girl before the sale took place."

"If it takes place, or so you said last night. Anyway, don't be so prim and proper. Come on, let's go in."

"How?" Is there a butler or someone looking after things?" he asked while peeking through the stained-glass of the front door.

"No, we're quite alone. But I have this for you."

Roger turned to see that the seductress had returned in all her splendor: the keys hung on their keyring which was hypnotically revolving round and round her finger as she leaned against one of the marble pillars. He moved to within inches of her scented body, took hold of the key and stepped back to the front door.

"When I'm sussing out an investment, everything else takes second place," he said with a grin that meant the matter was beyond dispute.

"If you're implying that you're saving the fun for after, then that's fine by me," she answered with a smile that meant the conversation had ended in a time-out.

Once inside, she had the chance to see for herself the luxurious lifestyle that the upper-crust lived, despite the bad times the Lady had fallen upon. She had, in fact, been there on another occasion, but only very briefly. Right now, her avid look was plain for Roger to see; like a wild animal stalking an easy press.

What her eyes saw was the opulent contents of a mansion built with all the lushness of a seventeenth century aristocrat, beginning with the stairs about eight or ten yards from the door and that divided into two halfway up towards the bedrooms.

They started, as is natural, with the living room where the tick-tock of a grandfather clock was the only sound to break the dusty silence.

"Doesn't the Lady have even enough money to pay for a cleaner?" asked Lilian scornfully, whilst dropping onto the ten-piece sofa. She liked how it surrounded the red-oak coffee table, under which she could feel a carpet that must have been brought from exotic and far-off lands, judging from the satin texture, as well as the elaborate designs sowed into it.

Roger looked to the left, where he could see the sports car through the convex windows – or concave, he thought, depending on your standpoint. In front of the window there was another skillfully carved table made of the same material. In the center stood what he felt sure to be a hand-painted vase.

"A shame it's empty," Roger said in a tone that showed the pity he felt for the owner. "Come on, let's continue."

They passed quickly through the dining room to the study on the other side of the hall. This was furnished from top to bottom with shelves of books which made Lilian ask the potential buyer if anyone would ever have taken the time to read them all. Roger didn't reply, but he was sure he knew one who might make an attempt at doing so; many of them were classical texts.

There was also a beautifully carved oak desk for working (or studying), a small chimney and finally what he took to be a brandy cabinet in one of the corners. All, in fact, extremely welcoming.

They came back to their starting point where Lilian unexpectedly took Roger's arm and rested her head on his shoulder.

"What do you think, darling? I think we and the kids would be very happy here, don't you agree? I'll have to learn to look after the garden, naturally."

"If I believe that, I'll believe anything. And let me warn you that I'm classed as an A1 skeptic."

"Oh, I see that you are beginning to get to know me."

"I'm glad to hear it," the banker said with pride – which was then laid to rubble by the replica.

"I´m not glad to have to say it, though; it´s a dangerous prospect! Come on, I´ll show you the kitchen and the ´back yard´.

She went ahead without waiting and the troubled businessman was again left wondering about Lilian´s topsy-turvy behaviour. What did she mean by her last puzzling comment? he was forced to ask himself. Did the possibility of getting close to someone frighten her?

Logically, he was musing over his talk with her father in which he referred to Lilian's mother's abandoning of her daughter. Then he had candidly, although maybe indiscreetly mentioned something about her shot-lived romances. Things were adding up, he surmised.

Suddenly he heard a familiar ´pop´. He left his thoughts behind and followed quickly after her. "We could have fun here, however," she said, handing him a glass of champagne.

The broker gladly took hold of the offering. "Are you really planning on staying around, then? Children excluded, of course."

"Don´t be so corny, Roger. And forget about all that romantic nonsense as well. Just enjoy what there is while you can. But yes, I can see myself living here -at least until it´s time to move on."

"You never will cease to give an ambiguous answer, will you?" he said, while feeling himself drawn irresistibly towards her. Lilian at once sensed his resistance begin to crumble and smiled in consequence.

"Anyway, the question is whether you are planning to stick around? Well, are you?" she asked, although by now neither the question nor the answer mattered to either of them.

"I haven´t decided."

"Then let me help you," she said, while slowly moving her scented figure towards him with overwhelming assuredness. "Why don´t you bring the bottle upstairs… and I´ll show you the bedrooms."

Yes, Lilian was now over the teasing game, while the last strands of Roger´s defenses willingly fell like the sandcastles he used to make as a child when the tide flowed over them, unstoppable. He lifted her in his arms and ordered *her* to grab the bottle and the glasses – which she did with relish.

What happened in the upper chambers was something that Roger had not foreseen. Not only was it something never experienced, it was unimaginable to him – until then. The only thing comparable was the occasion in which he had lost his footing in the sea as a child.

In contrast to the overwhelming wave of fear that caught hold of him then, now there was only a sense of release, of liberation, of dissolving into the blissful fusion with another whose own all-consuming desire for oblivion engulfed him again and again –and again once more.

Both succumbed to the pounding of each crashing wave of unrestrained giving; each time more willingly, each time with more urgency, unleashing themselves in answer to their so long repressed necessities without restraint, both entwined in a desperate discovery of one another.

When the raging storm fell into calm, Roger took some time to resurface from the depths of the sublime. He crawled to the surface like a castaway, then lay strewn upon the shores of a hitherto unknown paradise. When he finally opened his eyes, he saw that he was indeed alone, accompanied only by the yet intoxicating scent of rapture left behind after the shipwreck.

He pulled on his clothes and walked to the adjoining bathroom where he cleared his mind with a splash of cold water on his face. Refreshed and revitalized, Roger was whistling as he made his way back downstairs in search of Lilian.

As he reached the kitchen with the empty bottle and glasses, he looked through an opened window that gave onto the 'back yard', only to see her sitting motionless in the afternoon sun. She looked to be lost in thought, until he noticed her lips moving. When he freed his hands of their burdens and focused his attention on the scene outside, he indeed discovered that she wasn't thinking but talking to herself, repeating over and over the same phrase.

"I'm in control. I'm in control...."

Roger set to wondering: she might prefer for people to shower her with compliments about how pretty she was, but he still insisted on the attraction of the hidden side of her alluring personality. Some dark and murky, interior conflict was being fought, he felt sure.

Something was being repressed once again, and he believed he knew it to be one of two things: she was either unwilling to remain open to the consequences of the emotions that she had just shared with him - or was she unable to deal with them?

Was this beautiful flower blighted in some way, he continued asking himself. Was she so afflicted by her past that the cold, calculating side of her was trying to deceive her into not believing what she instinctively knew to be true? Namely, that what had happened between them had been more about the heart than the purely physical? That, in any case, was what he was feeling.

Then again, he told himself, trying to follow her advice on not being melodramatic, we all have our own subterranean waters flowing unseen to anyone, except perhaps the few who cross our path in life and show a little interest in drinking from them - if allowed. He had been so permitted, but would she consent to it happening again? That appeared to be the debate Lilian was having with herself, wasn't it?

"Only one way to find out," he said out load as he opened the back door noisily and faked a sudden appearance. The look that met his as he took a seat beside her reflected the policewoman's dark mood. It left the man no choice but to do what any other member of his sex would do at times like these: put his foot in it.

"Hey," he said in a foolish attempt at lightheartedness, "why don't we take a walk to the park and talk to Cynthia about her continuing to look after this place as well as her work in the park. I don't know where she finds the time, but she does one hell of a job." The poor soul even tried to end with a joke; "That way, you won't have to learn to look after the gardens, just give orders."

"Cynthia? Do you really think I'd go with you to see that viper? Why? So, you can compare the two of us? And as for working here, you'd just revel in that, wouldn't you? I could entertain you at night, and she during the day, is that it? She'd love that too. Skulking around here, waiting patiently for me to pack my bags and then install her own. What a nice little plan. You might have come up with a better story than the one of her working here: I know exactly how she spends her time."

Roger screwed his bewildered face, while trying to handle the vicious blow aimed at him.

"It's not something I made up, you know. I saw her entering the park through a gate that must be somewhere near here. And I saw her sleeping quarters in a little hut at the back of the greenhouses."

"I bet you did. And here was I telling myself that it was all purely Platonic. Round the back, eh?"

Roger struggled to recover his senses and wisely ignored the jealousy inspired comment. "But don't you see, the only reason she can have for sleeping there is that she is working for both the Town Park Department as well as for Lady Waverley. Why else would she be in and out of the two places, dressed in her gardener's outfit?"

"Did the friendly gardener tell you all of this," she asked with a level voice.

"No, like I said, I saw her coming out of the grounds here and into the park. She didn't see me and I didn't like to intrude into her private affairs. So I investigated a little, saw that the park shares a boundary with the estate and reached the obvious conclusion."

"Well, if you want some advice, don't ever go in for detective work; there are no obvious conclusions in our line of work. Secondly, just between friends, if you do buy this place, the park is also included, along with the zoo. They're both part of the estate."

"The mayor did mention that yesterday, as I'm sure you know. Are you implying something by it? So, what if Cynthia works exclusively for the Lady?"

"That's one way of putting it," Lilian laughed. "In any case, I'm only repeating what that lout of a politician said so as to make you think it through a little. For now, let me warn you that Lilian isn't the saintly sage from Alexandria that you think she is; she'd have probably burnt down the library before anyone else got the chance – and then blamed it on the barbarians."

"What are you saying? I thought you were friends. She did help in the murder investigation. You at least owe her that much."

"Is that what she told you, or is it another brilliant deduction of yours?"

"No, I heard it from her own lips."

"Well, well, well, so little Miss Philosophy told you, did she? And everything she says you naturally take as the god's truth, while everything I say is to be taken with suspicion, is that it? What kind of a relationship are we supposed to build on that basis? Tell me that!"

Before Roger had the time to refute her groundless affirmation, she stood up sharply. "I'm glad we've had this talk. It will make it easier for me to say goodbye. You can do as you wish as far as I'm concerned. Go home for good; come back and buy this place; take your precious Cynthia on as your personal gardener, lover, or wife – eventually. She won´t settle for anything less, I assure you."

"Lilian, can you please tell me where this is all coming from? Why this obviously unhealthy obsession with Cynthia?"

"I thought you were getting to know me. Figure it out. But while you do, you can do it without me."

Roger, despite the emotional upheaval he was undergoing, thought he had found his answer: although Lilian shrouded it with an unexplained polemic with Cynthia, the bottom line was that she wouldn´t permit him to get so close again –and he had foolishly given her the perfect excuse for doing so.

Chapter Nine

The woman who had been the cause of the row – or the excuse for it, as Roger believed – arrived at the park late that day and found him standing lost in thought, his unseeing eyes fixed on the gorillas. She wasn't dressed for her usual walk through the forest, so she had taken the bus all the way to the ′official′ entrance.

"It′s almost closing time," came her voice in his ear, having crept up stealthily from behind.

"Cynthia, I′m so glad to see you. And so prettily dressed, too. You look fantastic. What′s the occasion? Are you on your way into town for a romantic rendezvous? We can go together, if you like. To the town, I mean."

She explained that she had, as a matter of fact, just arrived from a meeting, not of the type referred to by Roger, but with the lawyer who was dealing with the last testament of a member of the family who had recently passed away. She was now on her way down to the office to change into her work-clothes.

Roger wasn′t fooled, though. "But you just said the place is about to close! You′re here so late in the day because you live in that little office, true?"

"Very astute, I must say. Although I don't sleep there every night. Only occasionally, as a matter of fact," she replied with her usual calm.

"It's also a fact that you look after the park here as well as the grounds on the other side of the fence, both of which form part of the same estate."

"You could say that," was her reply; almost a carbon copy of Lilian's answer to the same question – which struck the amateur detective as very odd. When he told Cynthia about it, she didn't appear to give it the slightest importance whatsoever and promptly directed the conversation towards what she was hungry to learn about. Namely, the details of everything else that had taken place since they last spoke.

So, Roger told her everything regarding the dinner with the mayor, his offer of acting as 'intermediary' over the sale of the estate, the conversation with Lilian that had ended the way it did only a few hours ago, and, last but not least, for his wanting to speak with her before making a decision. For obvious reasons, his story didn't include what had happened before his argument with the make-do estate agent.

"So, you'll be away for a few days and you want some of my comforting words of wisdom. Or is that you simply wanted to look upon me once more before you left?"

It was the first time that Roger had heard her say any sort of intimate comment, albeit a witticism, in terms of their relationship. He wandered whether it had a basis of truth to sustain it.

However it was, he could take it no further, as the zookeeper was calling time-up. Then Roger had a flash: why didn't Cynthia, already dressed for the occasion, join him for supper in town. It went without saying that he had to energetically reject her talk of being tired. A good relaxing glass of wine, he insisted, a nice meal made, served and cleared up by someone else was precisely what she needed. He would pay his part of the bill in cash and she in 'words of wisdom'. The stubborn gardener quickly came up with another excuse; she would have to come back here in the pitch black, which wasn't advisable.

"No problem," Roger counter-argued, she would sleep tonight in a soft bed in the hotel where he was staying.

She still hesitated. "Maybe it's not such a good idea. What will Lilian say if she finds out that you were dining with another woman, straight after your row and with this female in particular."

"That's ridiculous, and sexist. If you were a man, nobody would think twice about it. We're two friends eating out and chatting, that's all. The only difference is that the theme won't be on football. Come on, don't give it so much thought; be spontaneous," he finished with smile.

"You have me there. I can't go against my own silly advice, can I?" she joked in turn. "That would be like cheating on myself, as well as ruining my reputation, wouldn't it?"

They made their contented way to the exit and managed to catch the last bus to the hotel, where Roger promptly booked a room for Cynthia. He went to his own, washed and changed, and in no time at all was sitting next to the gardener who was waiting patiently at the cocktail bar at the entrance to the restaurant, looking over the menu. The smartly dressed young lady's ponytail swung first one way and then the other, as she greeted her host and then turned to the barman. She ordered two glasses of white wine and waited for Roger to get the conversation under way.

He began by telling her of his suspicions that Lilian had some obscure secret related to the new Mayor, his predecessor and all the circumstances surrounding the whole affair. Maybe it was a bad idea to get mixed up with them, both emotionally and with respect to the dubious sale of the Manor. As a matter of fact, he then went on to say, concerning Lillian's uncalled-for verbal attack, he now perceived some ulterior motive in the things she had said.

Cynthia's reply was to say that for one thing she wasn't a marriage guidance counselor, a joke that didn't have the desired effect on the worried trader. So, in a more serious tone, she simply repeated and that it wouldn't be right for her to defame someone who wasn't present to defend herself.

"You're too nice, Cynthia; or too prudent."

"That's as maybe, kind sir. In this, however, your praise is unmerited. I really can't see how I can help you."

"Let's me see, then," he said, gathering his thoughts for another attempt at unlocking this pretty philosopher's head. "You said something, or rather, you were on the verge of saying something about Lilian on our trek through the woods together, and then again during our walk together yesterday. I believe you have similar doubts about her that you preferred to keep to yourself. I'd like you to express those thoughts, despite your reservations about her not being here to confirm or deny them. I need some guidance. For starters, why didn't you strike up a real friendship?"

"Alright," she said, reluctantly giving in. "I'll give you my opinion, but only because you are in such a turmoil, and because I consider you a close friend who is worthy of trust. I always keep that word in mind when dealing with people."

"You can trust me as much as I trust you," Roger said sincerely.

"Thank you again for that. It's so necessary, isn't it? Apparently, that is the cause of your – of our – unease regarding Lilian. Anyway, here goes."

She began by talking about the bare facts surrounding the investigation that she had helped in, reiterating the fact that it remained, as yet, unresolved.

Roger shrugged his shoulders. "They never caught the culprit. So? Why do you attach such importance to it?"

She went on, explaining that because she had had a small hand in it, she had then followed, as best she could, what the police were doing to resolve the crime; newspapers, internet, chats with Jack and so on. In much the same way as had happened with Roger when he read the reports, it soon struck her as odd that the press should give so very little information, and even then only during the first day or two – after that, nothing. Even the amiable policeman was unable to say much after the initial days. It seemed the investigation was going nowhere and that the detectives involved weren't exactly losing sleep over it.

"And the head of the investigation was our Lily, right?"

"Now, Roger, I don't want you to start jumping to conclusions," she adverted him.

"Don't worry, I've already been warned against doing that today. In this case, though, why not? You seem to have done so, that's clear – or do you have other things to go on?"

"Well, after a few weeks the case was apparently shelved. Not 'officially' closed, just left on the pile of unresolved cases."

"Very strange," put in Roger, sipping his wine.

"The thing is, Lilian showed no signs of disappointment whatsoever at not finding the murderer; quite the contrary. Hence my decision to downgrade our incipient friendship - something she had no qualms about either, to tell you the truth."

Roger let fall the menu, the disbelief evident in his troubled voice.

"But do you believe Lilian capable of what I think you are getting at?" asked the not quite retired banker with growing apprehension. "That she was somehow involved? Or, if not directly, that she reaped some benefit after the fact by not getting to the bottom of it?"

"At first, no. Recently, however, events have renewed my suspicions. Take her career, for example. After such a failure with the case, you would expect it to have suffered a set-back, wouldn't you? Yet you've just told me that the new Mayor has gone and made her no less than the top-ranking officer in the police force. Apart from that, she runs the whole show at thirty-three years of age when there are good detectives, with a lot more experience, in line for promotion before her. And then…"

"And then? Go on," he almost demanded.

"I shouldn't really. What I was about to say involves you and your relationship with her. I'm afraid I was getting carried away."

Roger couldn't allow her to stop the train there. "You don't think I had a hand in the crime, do you?" he laughed, "I only got here last week."

"No, silly." Cynthia took Roger's hand and squeezed it gently. "This might hurt you."

The baffled young man took another sip of wine and asked her to go on, however it might affect his feelings.

"Very well. Let me ask you a question: you had never met the mayor before, right? And yet he invited you to the ceremony."

"On Lilian's insistence, I would imagine," Roger replied with a slow nod of his head.

"Exactly. Then he took you into his private office to persuade you to buy the Longstone Estate, including the zoo and the park I look after."

"Yes, but what are you getting at?" he asked, his impatience a sign of his growing interest.

"Who took you to look over the mansion?"

"Lilian, as you know."

"Now, at the risk of getting too personal, let me ask you; did the seduction continue? I mean, apart from enticing you to buy the place."

The guilty look on Roger's face was met by a smile that told of a suspicion confirmed. Cynthia carried on.

"Did she mention anything about you and her living there together, perhaps?"

"After her own fashion, yes."

"And later, you celebrated by, shall we say, inaugurating the sleeping quarters?"

Roger rubbed his stubbly chin while swirling the contents of the glass he was holding. After a few moments, he looked up.

"Are you insinuating that she somehow got to be the youngest chief of police in the country, not with any merit on her part, but by using some kind of 'subterfuge', even turning to crime? And that not content with what she'd achieved, she sees in my sudden arrival, a means of becoming the next Lady of the Manor?"

"Yes. I believe she is using you to further her already boundless ambition. Although, when it comes down to it, I'm only verbalizing the insinuations that you yourself made a moment ago."

They looked at one another in silence, hands still clasped.

"So much for my quest for happiness," said Roger with a sigh, immediately followed by a restrained laughter that they both shared.

"That's the spirit," Cynthia finally said. "Be patient. Today's bad experiences might be no more than the prelude to something great."

"Thanks for being with me when I needed you," was all that Roger could think of saying as way of gratitude.

"I just happened to be passing by, that's all. Anyway, it's getting late. I think I'll pass on the meal and call it a night," said the philosopher, standing up and straitening her clothes.

"I'll just finish the wine," Roger replied, "pay the bill and get off to bed as well. I'm catching the first train tomorrow. I'll give you a call… if I ever come back."

"Oh, you'll be back; you can't help but carry on seeking the happiness you're looking for, can you? And I'll be here waiting patiently as always. Just as I have done since I ran out on you in the ice-cream parlour."

She gave him the lightest of pecks on the cheek. "I'll go and get the keys. Room 205, wasn't it?"

Now Roger was left without words: Cynthia was the youngster who had had a crush on him without ever saying a word, not even her name? He watched her walk towards reception to retrieve the keys, the skirt she was wearing outlining her marvelous figure. His eyes followed her until she disappeared behind the lift doors.

Then a thought hit him: had she meant with her last phrase what he thought she meant? The hands, the kiss, the numbering of her room; was it a question or an affirmation? Had she subtly invited him to join her?

He scolded the reflection in the mirror on the wall behind the bar: "What are you thinking, Roger? Of doing just what Lilian had said you would end up doing? My god, Cynthia is a friend."

He shook his head. "I think you've had too much wine, my friend. Either that or you've lost your wits. In any case, Cynthia isn't the kind who would do what you just fantasized."

Chapter Ten

I'm taking the morning train with the normality that has characterized my decade and a half of commuting to and from the city. Today's hour long ride doesn't differ much from the ones I've made daily from the suburbs where I live into my workplace. Even so, on this occasion I feel out of sync with the rest of the passengers who have been incorporating their darkly suited corporeal forms to the common body of transients.

For one thing, I must be the only individual writing a diary; in which I feel the needy necessity of using the witty term 'mourning train' to describe the vehicle that is carrying them each to his own particular destination, once having alighted onto the platform teeming with others who are complying with the same hectic routine.

Roger closed his promising diary and laid his pencil to rest. In effect, his mood was probably less buoyant than when he set out on his 'quest' less than a week before, and in directions diametrically opposed – in more ways than one.

His head was in even more of a muddle than it had been then, while the only compensation for the complexities he had encountered were the vague, shadowy impressions of the happy child he had once had the fortune to have been. So ineffable were they that he couldn't even begin to describe them in his diary. The intricacies experienced in the flesh, however, were easily put down on paper.

In the first place, there was the turbulent affair (he didn't dare to qualify it as anything more profound) with the possibly corrupt policewoman, although he was having great difficulty in accepting the idea of her having a hand in the death of the former Mayor. There was, of course, the question of her rocketing career, which seemed not to end with being named the head of the police department, but to include becoming the new Lady of the Manor – with *his* necessary collaboration. If that were so, he asked himself while sitting on the train that would carry him home to some peace and quiet, it meant that their relationship was a farce with no possible future. And if *that* were so, what in heaven's name was he doing considering buying Longstone? What would he do there all alone? And by himself, to boot, he joked, but only half-heartedly.

With his inimitably comical misuse of the language, Cynthia automatically sprang to mind. Apart from her delightful sense of humor, she had also filled him with the hope of finding a direction, 'words of wisdom', but the philosopher turned gardener had also left him with doubts. Had she really made a pass at him the night before? It was another idea that he found hard to believe, but if it were so, was she truly the guiding sage he needed, or was she looking for something more than that between them? And if *that* were so, how was he to react?

She had certainly been right about one thing: in spite of everything, he couldn´t go back to his old life – just the train journey with the commuters had shown him that. But he had to overcome the fear of handing in his notice, which even now produced a tightening of his chest and a quivering of his legs. The idea went against all his upbringing, all he had been led to believe regarding the morals of working hard to make a living. And now there he was, just wanting to live! He smiled again, comforted by the idea that fortunately for him, he could always fall back on his whimsical wordplay to lighten his moods.

In what seemed like no time at all, he had reached his stop, ´unparked´ the car he had left in the small car park and re-parked it in the driveway of his house. He dropped his small travel bag in the hall and went in search of his cell phone. The first thing to do was to call his mother; seeing that the famous postcard didn´t reach the person to whom it was supposed to have been directed to, he thought it the right thing to do.

She began, as was her custom, by saying that she wouldn´t allow Roger to just say a few niceties over the phone and therefore insisted on him seeing her face to face – as any dutiful son should. The fact was that she had no motive for complaint, given that her considerate offspring had already booked a table for seven-thirty at her favorite restaurant. It was where she had met and dined with her late husband on most special occasions. She thanked him as warmly as any grateful mother would, she ended with her habitual but always well-meant irony -or so it seemed from her point of view.

In the meantime, the banker went for a trim at his local hairdressers, more than anything just to say his last farewells. After so many monthly chats, he didn´t want to simply vanish. His kind disposition was rewarded with a free haircut and a genuinely heart-felt hug from the middle-aged woman who had made his hair presentable in public for more than a decade.

As he was leaving, Roger suddenly asked her who was going to do such a good job in the future. It hadn´t been easy to find someone who knew exactly the style he wanted.

"Finding a wife will be child's-play compared", were her last words. The handsome broker didn´t know how to respond that one. Little did he know that his dinner-guest would provide him with an answer.

He met her at the appointed hour. Roger talked most through the meal, astutely avoiding the ´unnecessary details´ that might be embarrassing or cause a prejudgment on his mother's part. When he had finished, Florence - as the woman who had gladly carried him around in an ambience of amniotic pleasure for nine enjoyable months - sat back with one of those motherly smiles that told her precious son that his cleverness wasn't at all worthy of self-praise.

"So," she began," if I'm not mistaken, after all of these years of not finding someone to share your life with, you suddenly have two suitors."

"There's no fooling you, is there mother? I shouldn't have tried, anyway. Sorry. But about what you said, I don't think 'suitors' is the word I would use to describe the situation."

"A little old fashioned, I know, but changing the word won't change the world; people are the same as they have been since Adam bit into the fruit," she said with assuredness.

"It was Eve who tempted him."

"Is that supposed to mean that you believe one of the two ladies to be enticing you to swallow the idea of buying this country estate?" Florence asked.

"The evidence does seem to point in that direction," he answered with a sigh.

"I don't see why you've reached such a bitter conclusion, son. If you are in love with one another, then it's only natural that your future wife should look for a 'nice place' to raise a family. Neither is it something out of the ordinary to want the best you can afford. I did exactly the same when I married you father, although our income never gave for too many luxuries. As you recall, the reason you spent so many occasions holidaying in the same town is that your auntie, god bless her soul, invited us there every summer. Yes, if I were in her shoes, I'd be encouraging you to buy the estate; lock, stock and barrel – or should I say gorillas?"

His mother's perceptiveness always left Roger pleasantly stunned. How could she in any way know anything about the possible relationships that he had formed from the little he had told her, however clumsily he might have done so? "You know, mum, you and Cinthia have the same uncanny knack of guessing at what I haven't said and getting it right.

"Son, I've known you since before you were born," she said offhandedly.

"Well, I congratulate you on you being such an attentive mother, but I'd like to get back to when you said that bit about being in love. Which of the two are you thinking of, because even I don't know who I'm in love with, much less the fact that it's corresponded!"

"Well Lilian, of course. Now don't make another foolish attempt at trying to convince me otherwise. You are both caught – hook, line and sinker."

Roger took -which is not to say he accepted- the affirmation with as much composure as he could. "Is that so?"

"Without a doubt; and I'm glad for you – maybe I'll soon get to be a grandmother after all," she said rubbing her hands together delightedly, as if the matter was a foregone conclusion. Judging by her following words, it was: "So tell me, son, what do you have in mind employment-wise? I imagine the mansion and the grounds will cost a bit to look after, what with the staff and taxes and all the rest of it. Apart from the fact that it's a long way from your present job."

"Hold on a second," he said to his imaginative mother, with the first sign of frustration creeping in. "Don't you think you're going a little too fast? You may see a wedding and children ahead. I don't."

"Let's leave those things aside, then, and suppose that you buy the place and live there in unhappy solitude. How would you make ends meet?"

"That's more sensible," Roger said, deciding to play the game of make-believe landowner, while getting one back on the exasperating woman who had given birth to him. "The fact is that, come what may regarding everything we've talked about, I've already decided to leave the company."

"Oh, I see," she said sarcastically, "that seems like a great idea; simply give up your career, throw away fifteen years of your life and sit gazing at those gorillas while your savings run out?"

"When they do, do you think that Lilian will still love me?" he asked in the same sarcastic vein as his mother.

"That's a blow below the belt, Roger. Now answer the question; it is probably the most important thing you'll ever have to decide upon."

"My salary is only a portion of what I earn. If it suits me, I can sit gazing at the gorillas, as you flawlessly put it, while handling my own investments on my laptop. There is also......"

Florence watched her son's face light up, which told her that her question was about to receive an answer. "There is also what?" she prompted.

"Mum, it's virtually impossible to get to see these animals in their homeland in Africa, so don't you think people would come to see them living out their lives in their *natural habitat* – or as close to it as is possible – practically just down the road from where we are right now? Listen, the last Mayor had already begun the construction of such an area, which would be surrounded by camouflaged glass that viewers could see through without being seen by the gorillas – before he hit some problem that no-one seems clear about. That doesn't matter now, however, because... I could close the zoo down and, together with some of the estate's other grounds, turn the project into reality."

"Give up everything to look after gorillas? Ludicrous!" his mother snorted.

"Equally ludicrous is the idea of my marrying Lilian," he retorted defensively. "If anything, Cynthia would be the ideal wife; she knows everything green. Anyway, that's not what we're talking about, is it? Where was I? Oh yes: don't you see? The people would pay for the pleasure, adding to my income. The town would also be boosted economically and most important of all, the gorillas would have a safe, natural haven."

Seeing the tremendous passion with which her son spoke about the project, the limitless love she felt for him made her antagonism towards his plan disappear: the only thing she wanted was for him to be happy.

"O.K., son, I'm not one for business, so I'll trust in your good sense. I still insist, though; you're not in love with Cynthia."

Roger gave her a tender smile. "You can't possibly know that."

"Listen, Roger, we don't choose a life-long partner because we think he or she can look after the garden. It's not very romantic, but it's exactly what you've just said."

The meal ended and Roger took her home in a taxi, which then continued to his own residence. There he excitedly switched on his computer and began studying everything he needed to know on how to set up and run the home he envisaged for his gorillas – and for those to come.

In spite of the late night, he jumped out of bed next morning with an enthusiasm he hadn't experienced since…. his childhood! He took his diary to mark down this exceptional start to what would be a remarkable day. He broke his fast after the indispensable dawn ritual in front of the open windows, then headed into the city center and the office whose employees were going to receive the stunning news of their bosses' renouncement.

For some reason, he made a point of letting them all know before contacting the board of directors at the headquarters of the multinational in Boston, USA. Maybe that way he would have burned his last bridge; crossed the Rubicon; or been up the creek without a paddle!

His transatlantic announcement was met with surprise, shock, and even some reprimands for the abruptness of it. All of which he dealt with fearlessly and calmly: yes, the fear had vanished unnoticed the night before, swept away by the thrill of the adventure awaiting him. He now knew clearly what it was, what it had been, and what it always would be that he wanted, at least as far as the animals were concerned; the human factor was another thing altogether.

There was one last anchor to be raised prior to unfolding his sails and setting a course for the little port awaiting him: the selling of the house that had never really been a home.

Once again, the task was done with consummate ease. He simply paid a visit to the real estate office where he found the agent who had handled the purchase very professionally. He dropped the keys on his desk and, in front of his astonished face, told him the price he wanted for it. Then he turned and headed for the door.

"Mr. Penrose," called a deep voice in reclamation, "you are going to entrust me with your property, just like that? I could hire a van tomorrow and clean the place out."

"Mr. Collins, the day I can no longer confide in my own judgement of character, will be the day I'll go and live on a desert island."

The feeling, although not the phrase itself, was genuinely his: he felt as confident in himself as he was carefree.

Chapter Eleven

The now definitively out of work financier was scrutinizing the zoo, surveyor's maps in hand – provided by the town hall's urban development department – the following week. He had, in fact, spoken to the mayor on the day he had paid his last visit to the workplace, a conversation in which the politician had accepted with enthusiasm Roger's decision and had expressed no qualms over the buyer's one and only condition: that of being granted the license for his project. It would be presented and, no doubt about it, authorized by the corresponding department as soon as he could arrange it.

As the Mayor had "guaranteed" the motion being passed without a hitch, he naturally got to work; with his new outlook so free from care, he saw no reason to worry over political nuances.

Just as he had begun unrolling the blueprints, his attention was drawn to the long expected, slender figure swaying towards him. Nothing, however, could stop the sudden pounding of his heart and the butterflies in his stomach. And yet, despite the memory of his mother's words, his head refused to accept the effect as anything other than pure animal desire, and *that* he could tame.

"I thought I'd find you here," said Lilian, as cheerfully as the pleasant sunny day that the late spring had gifted them with. Her good humor was sincere and unadorned, as was her semblance; the bare minimum of make-up, her hair tied neatly behind, and her clothing simple but elegant. Under more convivial circumstances, Roger would have told her that even a sack would grace her, but he held fast.

"I thought you'd find me here, and I'm no policeman," he said in cold contrast.

"Don't I know it. But you are certainly going to be the best dressed zookeeper in the country."

Despite his initial reaction, her bubbling voice made him want to cradle her in his arms, to protect her from the dangers of her hazardous job, to listen to her telling him of her fears, her hopes, dreams, secret wishes - and of how much she cared for him.

He continued fighting against the urge; he wouldn't allow himself to be beguiled by the Sunday morning version of whom he believed to be the ambitious, unscrupulous person hiding behind it. Lilian went on speaking.

"You know, if you built a tea or coffee shop up there at the entrance, it would be a good place for someone silly like me to invite someone special like you to sit and have a chat. Ideal, in fact, for apologizing - and forgiving the said silly person's behavior."

What Roger was about to say in response became suddenly much more difficult than the many times he had imagined. The apparently bare sincerity of her words, not to mention the tender look in her eyes, left him momentarily unable to vocalize. He swallowed saliva to moisten his parched throat.

"I'm not sure I can forgive you. I'm not even sure if I want to. I think you're behavior the other day made it plain to see that your only interest in me is to further your plans of climbing the social scale by the use of any means at your disposal – myself included."

"My plan? What plan? And what do you mean exactly? Do you think I'm using you in some way?" she asked, the hurt visible in her salt-watery eyes.

"Why deny it?" he persisted, "the case of the deceased Mayor was a complete failure, and yet his successor makes you the chief of police. Why would he do such a thing? By the way, it was him I saw you with in the hotel restaurant, wasn't it?"

"So, you think we are in league to take over the town? That we're lovers? That we're guilty of covering up the murder? Or are you saying that we executed the whole thing?"

"You tell me."

"No, you tell me just exactly what you think."

Roger maintained his silence, watching how Lilian, wounded and upset, took a deep breath before plunging into her defense.

"Look, the investigation was a pantomime, but not because of me; the case was taken from my hands, shortly after I began to follow the lead of the exotic flower found in his clenched fist. To tell you the truth, I was dismissed immediately after speaking to someone who knows all there is to know about that kind of flower."

Roger looked at her sharply but said nothing. Lilian didn't yet follow up on what she was driving at but took up another argument.

"As for the promotion, I'm as much in the dark as you are. You saw me with the mayor because he asked me to dine with him to give me the news in person, before making it public. If you really want to know, he did make an attempt at what you were hinting at, but I went home to bed that night alone."

Unconvinced, Roger carried on with his argument. "Wasn't it strange, nonetheless, that he should invite me to the ceremony where he conveniently took me aside to talk about buying the estate? Promising me, a complete stranger, all the help he could in the process. After which it was you in person who took me to see the house, and who talked about us being happy there together. You made good use of your multiple personalities as it suited you in every moment."

"Right, then," said the detective, feet apart and hands on her hips. "I killed the former Mayor with the connivance of who was to become his successor; then he named me the chief of police; needless to say, I jumped into bed with him (when his wife wasn't around); then I cleverly used him to get you to buy the mansion, dumped him and seduced you with the aim of becoming the next Lady of the Manor."

"That sums it up pretty well; are you willing to sign a written confession?" he answered, his tone verging on the needlessly brutal.

The policewoman now showed signs of exasperation. "But that's not how it is; I didn't do any of those things that you are accusing me of. I put criminals behind bars, and I don't give my body away as if it were a headless doll."

She paused a moment, and then continued with her counterattack.

"While we're on the subject of accusations, where did you get these ideas about me from? Who put them into your head?"

Her growing anger forced her into leaving her initial prudence aside. "And let me tell you something else about the case that might interest you: I didn't come to the park looking for Cynthia's help; that was a ruse. I came to watch her as closely as possible without raising her suspicion!"

The look of disbelief that took hold of Roger's face informed her of her mistake without the necessity of hearing the proceeding words. Indeed, attacking Cynthia, for as much as Lilian might be in the right, was counterproductive. It had only hardened his posture, to the extreme of his ignoring the obvious question as to the evidence she might have to back up what she had just affirmed.

"What suspicion?" he said vehemently. "Is Cynthia to blame now? Apart from the idea being insane, she's not the one who enticed me into making the investment in the house, as well as turning it into our home; you did."

In the wink of an eye Lilian's anger faded, leaving bare the pain that she had always feared, and that she had so cleverly avoided; until now. Roger saw how her tears began to fall irresistibly while her crestfallen voice, as well as the words it conveyed, were like a torture.

"Of course I did," she said quietly, wiping away her silently, gently falling tears. "I did so because I love you. I've always loved you. And I've been waiting for you ever since I pushed the ice-cream cone into your face and ran out. I hid around the corner of the shop waiting for you to come after me... but you never did. Your parents arrived and took you away. Then I waited every summer for you to return... but you never did," she finished, repeating the same phrase with infinite sadness.

Roger had to turn his back on her, trying desperately to maintain both his physical composure and his internal stance. Despite feeling his heart being wrenched from him, his following words could only be described as one of those occasions when we deceive ourselves into believing that what we are doing, or saying, isn´t what we know deep down to be terribly wrong; and yet, we continue.

"Now I know you´re lying. You aren´t the girl in the ice-cream parlor. It was Cynthia; she already told me so. I´m sure your tears are as false as your words. Please leave me."

Despite her moisture laden eyes, Lilian turned and, with her head held high, walked silently away. Not of her own free will but obliged by the man who had refused to accept her apologies for what she had done. One thing he couldn´t do, however, was to make her get down on her hands and knees. She could have finally given away her heart, but not her dignity.

Roger remained with his back to her dwindling figure; he was acutely aware of what he had done, yet couldn´t bear the sight of seeing her leave him... forever? Although the sun was shining, the perturbed investor´s skin was wrapped in a cold sweat, while the pounding in his chest went on and on. A while later he was found by the head gardener, looking in the direction of the gorillas, his sight lost in the infinite space that too often separates all human hearts.

"Roger," Cynthia said with her usual unshakable calm, "I'm pleased to see you once again. Or perhaps I should put that on reserve; you look upset. What's wrong? Has something happened to the gorillas? Hey, are those the zoo reforms you're holding? I've heard about your new home for the gorillas. Can you show me the plans?"

"I'd rather not right now, if you don't mind. I have a better idea; do you have anything to drink in that little shack of yours?"

Roger downed a first swift glass of white wine, re-filled his glass and began to tell of his encounter with Lilian. His philosophical friend soon made a gesture for him to stop. The details were unnecessary, she said. Her knowing them wouldn't help anyone.

"You are too nice, as I've said before," was his mumbled reply. He had just made vanish his third round. "Well, let me tell you about a less bitter meeting, the one I had with my mother. Do you know what? She said that, apart from being crazy doing what I'm doing, I should marry Lilian."

"Did she indeed? And how did you reply?"

"I said that I would be better off marrying you."

The gardener laughed. "I think you´ve had enough wine for today – not to mention emotions. You must be tired. I don´t know about the alter, but I can get you to the bus stop on time. You go back to the hotel and have a lie down."

"You´re right. You´re always right. From now on I´ll do whatever you advise, go wherever your advice takes me. By the way, did I tell you about quitting my job? You weren´t wrong about that either. I have no more fear."

"I´m glad to hear it, as well as about having you back again. Welcome home," she finished, looking into his eyes and taking his hand. "Now, to the bus. I´ll see you tomorrow, and maybe you can show me those blueprints."

When tomorrow came, he was back at the front with the first of an army of experts of every type who would guide him on his way to becoming a keeper of gorillas. When tomorrow went, he was the proud owner of the Waverley Estate; the mayor was certainly gaining his stripes, too.

So, during the warm summer months of learning and forgetting, he was in constant and unremitting contact with botanists and naturalists; with surveyors, architects and builders; with Town Hall planning department bureaucrats, along with their colleagues from the department of tourism; and finally, as if he were a travelling-show juggler, he had many a chat with Oliver, the long-standing zookeeper, who would naturally remain until his age, or his back pains would allow.

The new owner had grown fond, as well as respectful of, the aging chatterbox, to the effect that together they would be responsible for overseeing the closing down of the installations, which naturally meant the as comfortable as possible change of residence of the rest of the animals. Their joint collaboration would see to it that they all finished their days in some kind of national park, where they would be well looked after – and as free as the circumstances allowed.

By the end of the August, Roger calculated, they would all be gone to their new homes and the cages that had imprisoned them for so long torn down to make way for the change of face of the whole area. The zoo extension in itself wasn't big enough to play home for the gorillas' new habitat, as was reflected in the plans he finally handed in to the local government for their approval. He had the mayor's word that there would be no hitches, but the agility of officialdom was always to be doubted.

It was, in fact, the only thing needed to get the project underway: the new fauna demanded by the scientists was already on its long journey from Africa, the contracts for landscaping had been drawn up and needed only to be implemented.

In the meantime, publicity was also being drawn up based on the projected marvel. The first prototype pamphlets were delivered to the as yet potential gorilla park owner. The visitor's wouldn't begin arriving until the following spring, according to all the estimations, but his way of doing things had always been to be ready to give the go ahead to any operation well in advance.

On precisely the last Friday of August, the month that should have seen the departure of the last of the other animals, he took a variety of the fliers home with him to get someone else's opinion.

Chapter Twelve

The relationship between Cynthia and Roger had steadily grown beyond that of acquaintances into something closer, although as yet purely platonic, never better said. Between walks and talks in which the increasingly expectant landlord shared many of his life experiences, she had at first moved from her hut in the park to taking over the quarters in the summer house, then from there to sharing the mansion with Roger, each to their own sleeping quarters.

He insisted on hiring a proficient landscape gardener to look after the estate, while Cynthia's time was taken up ever increasingly with the overseeing of the refurbishment of the country house. However, she wouldn't submit to Roger's suggestions about leaving the upkeep of the park to someone else; she never stopped insisting that her park was also her creative sanctuary.

In effect, there had been no open signs between the two of going beyond the present relationship. Rather, in some inexplicable fashion, Roger, at least, assumed that the flower that had been planted would typically blossom one day soon into what everyone in town already took for granted -or so it had reached his ears. It was nature left unto herself, they said. As is the way of things, even the Garden of Eden wasn't free from its own endemic imperfections. Despite all of our well laid plans, flaws would naturally show up, leading to their own destined outcome as if they had a will of their own.

For example, the 'quest' for happiness that Roger had undertaken, and that had led to him being on his way to his new stately home, publicity in hand and looking forward to sharing his evening meal with his philosophical, green-fingered partner, hadn't quite crystallized into the blissful state he had hoped for. He had no complaints, certainly; to all intents and purposes he was esteemed by all to be the luckiest guy on earth. And yet....

And yet he hadn't reached the point where he could be seen – as he had been as a child – walking around the streets whistling, even singing, out load; no-one had as yet found it necessary to baptize him as 'the smiler'; and he was still unable to say with his hand on his heart that his mind was free from all worries or regrets - which was, after all, what the seaside trip had been all about.

He wasn't consciously thinking about all of this as he walked home with the leaflets, but he soon would.

"Hello Cynthia," he shouted as he entered, "how is my little lighthouse of Alexandria?"

"Shining brightly, complying with her function of keeping dangers at bay," Cynthia called back jovially.

"How are things at the Gorilla Park? Any news about the building permit? The delay is most complexing," she continued as she appeared from the kitchen, wooden spoon in hand -today was one of the chef's days off. "And what are those things you're carrying? Holiday brochures? Are you planning the honeymoon already?" She too appeared to have heard the amusing town gossip.

Roger answered that she was right about the holidaying part, but that she was wrong about their purpose. He offered her the brochures and she a glass of wine, their hands touching in the process. Suddenly, the air seemed to fill with vibrant energy. They looked at one another intensely, silently swallowing the elixir while exchanging age old messages that both now knew would be answered.

Without a word Cynthia finally unleashed the passion that had been artificially subdued since the night in the hotel, when her subtle inference had been ignored. The new estate owner gladly recognized that he had been right all along, letting loose his glass and embracing the fire awaiting him, ready to be burnt at the stake for his sins.

When the flames subsided some time later, each slipped on one of Roger's housecoats and made their way downstairs amidst chuckles of laughter and playful embraces. Roger went to the kitchen to get two more glasses of wine with which to quench the thirst brought on by the afternoon heat, in both senses of the word. He received a titillating smile full of promise as he handed the glass to the resplendent woman sitting on the lounge-room sofa; the fire was only left smoldering, not extinguished.

Meanwhile, she had picked the publicity leaflets from the hall floor where she had let them fall and was about to flip through them, so that Roger took his place beside her in order to look them over together.

All seemed to meet with her approval until she opened one that had a small map of the park superimposed on the surrounding area. She put down her glass and asked a simple question in a tone that hinted at some kind of affront; well concealed, but not well enough.

"Is this the intended site to be constructed?" was the abrasive question aimed with subtle ill-intention at the man with an arm perched affectionately on her shoulder.

"Yes. The naturalists tell me it´s quite large enough. Do you see any problem at all?"

Cynthia´s half-hearted attempt at being tactful was promptly forgotten as a previously unseen wave of irritation took hold of her gentle demeanor, leaving it in tatters on the living room floor.

"Yes, I certainly do. The naturalists can go take a jump. Do you see any problem at all with *that*?" she replied with a grin that was obviously in open disagreement with her words. She stood up, gave the puzzled and disappointed young man an ominous kiss on the cheek and made her haughty way back towards the kitchen.

He mechanically went to help, but the teamwork that they had forged over the last months wasn't like it had been.

"But what was normal?" he suddenly asked himself, his own little lighthouse light having lit up. It was impossible to tell: he didn't really know enough about the woman to say what was normal in her or not. He took a bottle of wine and scrutinized the label.

"You know, Cynthia, if you don't mind me changing the subject for a moment -and if you'll excuse the terrible exaggeration- I've just been thinking. I probably know more about the contents of this bottle than I do about your early childhood, not to mention adolescence, which is, I suppose, when your projected career started to form in your mind – never better said. My fault, of course. I've been so absorbed in my own personal problems, my 'quest ', the gorillas, the house, and so on. We have chatted a lot during these last couple of months, but we haven't spoken much about you. So, it's high time to make amends, don't you think? Tell me how you came to be a philosopher and how you came not to be a philosopher; that is, of the radical change of course that led you to living and sleeping – almost quite literally – on a flower bed. You did promise to, if I stayed around. Remember? The first day in the park?"

"Of course; and I was wondering when you were going to ask," she answered sarcastically -which was another sign that things were taking an unexpectedly bitter turn. "Anyway, not to be worried at, is it? Where do I begin?"

"Well," Roger said with utmost care not to say the wrong thing as on previous occasions, "apart from what I've just mentioned, there is something that intrigues me; you're from this town... and yet you don't speak like the others. I mean, apart from your erudition, your accent is totally different."

Cynthia sighed as if she were already bored talking about herself but felt obliged by the circumstances to continue. She began by explaining that at the age of five she had left the town – the country, in fact – to go and live in Switzerland. From there, at the age of sixteen, she went to the United States to take up her studies in philosophy, before coming back to England to do her PhD. After a few years in the world of academia, she began to find it stale, even – dare she say it – boring. Then she thought of her home with all of its vibrant fecundity, so unlike the stagnant pond of sterile contemplation.

"So, home I came to take part in the process of planting seeds and watching them grow into something beautiful, something of my own creation. I felt the need to dig my fingers into the earth, get my feet stuck in the mud and," she said finishing with an encouraging touch of humor," to let the rain fall gently on my sodden hair."

"And your parents? Are they still living abroad?"

"No. My mother died when I was three, my father five or six years ago." She finished her story with a perplexing phrase; "You see, he could live and die without his daughter, but he couldn't without this stuff." She signaled the glass of alcohol in her hand, the inference brutally plain to see by the grief on her face.

"I'm sorry to hear that," Roger answered, showing his compassion. After a short silence he made an attempt at lightening the atmosphere. "So, after moving around Europe and the USA, you finally decided to come back to look after this place. Is that the reason for your disapproval of the gorilla park? It alters things in a way you don't like? I see that you've grown fond of these lush woodlands and green lawns."

He thought he now understood her anger on seeing the plans: he had no idea of how wrong he was, and he had seen nothing yet as far as her change of personality was concerned. It hit him like a thunderbolt thrown at him by Zeus in person.

"Allow me to fill in the gaps of my life, then maybe you'll begin to see what this estate means to me," she began again, her voice slowly climbing in intensity. "I didn't *go* to Switzerland; I was sent to school there by the same drunkard who left what should have been my inheritance in financial ruin. I came back to fulfill the promise he made to my dying mother of taking care of it all, intact, just as it has been for the last three centuries."

Although she moved closer, the decibels kept rising, leaving Roger's mind ringing in disconcert.

"*I* am Lady Eleanor Sofia Cynthia Waverley, you blind fool, and despite the fact that you bought my ancestral home with your rags to riches money, you'll never have the slightest inkling of what my feelings are – and you are not going to overrun half of my lands with gorillas. Is that clear?"

She could have said it neither louder nor clearer. It had penetrated through the shock of what had been revealed of her past, as well as her present. The future, Roger would have to leave for another day; right there and then he was so dumbfounded that any kind of rationalizing was beyond his ability, or, for that matter, his desire. Things had taken a turn that had once again drawn him into a numbing bewilderment. On one thing he had to agree, however; he was as shortsighted as a mole.

Chapter Thirteen

The distraught owner of Longstone was forced to spend the weekend alone, although he couldn't say that he regretted the fact. It gave him time to recover from the dramatic outburst of rage that Cynthia had subjected him to. After the ensuing night of silent tension, he had risen to find a small note on the kitchen table. It was a written apology for her unforgivable behavior and for her coming absence, signed with a small drawing of a lighthouse.

He wandered over the creaking floorboards, going from silent room to silent room of her ancestral home, while trying to assimilate the new perspective of what he had thought of as *his* future home, product of the enormous change of character of the Lady who should have been the heiress. He couldn't find it in him to blame her for her behavior, however. The tragic loss of both her parents, and now her estate, must indeed have been bitter blows. If truth be told, he marveled at the composure she had shown, as well as her kindness towards him. No wonder she hadn't been able to make friends with Lilian, suspecting of her what she suspected, he told himself.

The weather had also varied from several days of sunshine to a weekend of rain that today was being swept around by the bothersome blustery winds, making the umbrella that he carried with him on a stroll outside, of no use whatsoever.

Back indoors, he did some cooking, read a little from one of the library's collection of books, spent some time in internet and watched a couple of documentaries on TV, as well as a film on the classic channel. He also kept his diary, in which on this occasion he unfortunately failed to maintain the touch of humor that had been its distinctive trait. He wrote mostly of reconsidering his friendship with Lady Waverley – not that her identity made a difference, it was a question of his misguided trust in her. What else hadn't she told him?

When Monday finally came dragging its feet, the restless investor decided to head into town to have a chat with the mayor about the license to start the necessary reforms. Cynthia hadn't come home, nor had she contacted him. Sooner or later, they would have to talk over her stance on the plans: although he wasn't willing to make concessions, he still had to smooth out the troublesome issue in some way that he was as yet unable to envisage.

The rain had moved out to sea towards the continent, so that he took the convertible Porsche Spider, which he parked along the waterfront from where he would walk to the Town Hall in a question of minutes. After taking no more than a few steps in the direction of his projected destination, he came across none other than the friendly policeman who had rescued him from the rain on that night... so long ago.

"Hello Jack, great to see you again," he said eagerly. "Taking the sun, are we?"

The sun seeker greeted his friend with the same delight. "It's been a few months since we've spoken; I suppose you are busier than a bee, what with the animals, the house - and the wedding."

"Wedding? What wedding?" he responded rhetorically, knowing exactly to what Jack had alluded.

"Your marriage to Cynthia. It's common knowledge," he said defensively, "I don't want you to take me for a gossiping busybody."

"I don't. Just as I don't know who could have started the absurd rumor; it certainly wasn't me. Anyhow, tell me what you've been up to with your free time – it is difficult adjusting to a new lifestyle, isn't it? And your daughter, how is she doing in her new role? I bet she's enjoying telling everyone what to do."

"Hmm," Jack kind of laughed, "I don't know about that. Oh yes, she always did like bossing people around – part of her loveable character." Roger looked at him sideways but was satisfied with letting Jack carry on with his account of what was happening.

"To tell you the truth," he said somewhat gloomily, "she doesn't seem to be too satisfied with things – with her life in general, I mean to say."

"Why do you say that?" asked Roger, powerless to conceal his interest.

"She's a bit down in the dumps, if you must know. More than a bit, as a matter of fact - but you didn't hear it from me, you understand? To tell you the truth – and I think you worthy of my trust – if I didn't know any better, I'd say she was heartbroken; I recognize the symptoms."

"Oh, really?" commented his listener with reticence, unsure about digging deeper into Lilian's personal situation. Even he, as stubborn as he was, couldn't deny his desire to know, but he had the foreboding that it would lead to compromising himself.

"The thing is," Jack continued, "I can't remember her going out with anyone for a good while; if she did, she kept it a secret. It used to be a bit of a joke between us; I'd ask her when she was going to get married and give me some grandchildren, her answer being that she would – as soon as she found the right man for her children and the right man for a husband."

"Yes," Roger let out, "she said the same thing to me during our first meal together."

"And when was that?" Jack asked only half surprised. "She never mentioned it. Neither did you, come to think of it."

"Eh… the night before the promotion ceremony."

"The ceremony to which you were invited, for some unknown reason – or so it appeared at the time. It was also the night before she took you to look over the estate. I thought that a bit queer at the time, but now it begins to make some sense."

"Jack, do you remember the postcard I wrote on the day I came here?"

"Never forget it. Did the person in question ever show up?"

"He's… still on his way. But one of the requisites of his making it, so I've been told, is to be sincere – with myself and my friends."

"Go on," said the retired policeman to the retired financier with resignation. "Something big is coming my way, I reckon."

"I believe you've guessed what it is, too, haven't you? I'm responsible for Lilian's torment."

Roger, true to his word, went into the details – leaving out only the strictly intimate. When he had finished, his friend took out the pocket watch he had received from the hands of the mayor, thoughtfully opening and closing it for a few minutes. At last he spoke.

"Well, well. Lilian suspects Cynthia of being involved in some way or another with the death of the previous Mayor, while Cynthia thinks the same about my Lilian. Just to add spice to the sauce, you came along. Anyhow, it appears to be one of two things: or my daughter is a criminal, or my ´adopted´ daughter is. Either way, it´s hard to believe," he finished in a low voice.

Roger asked the sergeant how he could take their possible guilt without blowing a fuse.

"Simple, son. You see, I only said that it *appears* to be. You, on the other hand, are taking for granted that one of the two is in the right. Haven´t you considered the chance that they are both wrong about the identity of the culprit?"

"Why of course," said the younger man with evident relief. "Neither of them is responsible; I couldn´t really believe it of them either."

"Now, now," Jack went on in his professional style, "It´s only an occurrence of mine, something to ponder over, if you like. Anyway, leaving aside the crime itself, there is another question that remains unanswered."

Roger was warming to the task of playing detective. "What are you getting at?" he asked eagerly.

"One of the two is a liar – and that's a fact. They can't both be the girl who pushed the ice-cream into your face."

"Obviously not; but apart from grilling them down at the police station, I can't think of how to get the guilty party to confess."

"That's because you aren't a policeman," said Jack with an accompanying wink.

Roger's enthusiasm suffered a little at his friend's comment and he answered in consequence. "Which means you're telling me, in your own indirect manner, that *you* are; ergo that *you* have the solution. Correct me if I'm wrong," he finished a little haughtily.

"Not at all; your deduction is faultless," he replied, generously throwing the peeved would-be policeman a propitious compliment. "As for what to do, you simply get out your telephone, send a message to each of them saying that you have something important to show them and ask them to meet you at the ice-cream parlour. I say them, but the one mustn't know about the other's invitation, you understand."

Roger thought for a moment. "The problem is that I don't remember the name of the place, and there are quite a few in town. Neither of them will be able to come."

"You still haven't caught on, have you?" responded the policeman. "The one who is lying won't be able to come; the one who telling the truth will know where it is without you telling her the name or the address." Jack, always true to his old-fashioned self, added, "Whoever shows up is the girl for you!"

"What a good plan; why didn't I think of it?" said Roger, adding quickly, "Now don't answer that!"

Chapter Fourteen

The following morning found Roger, once having completed his morning ritual in one of the upstairs rooms that looked onto a narrow strip of the distant grey sea, now standing alone in the spacious kitchen, coffee in hand, thinking over Jack's solution. Not that he had any doubts about putting it into action, the question was one of timing.

Cynthia – the Lady of the House - had finally deigned to contact him, notifying him as to her mid-morning arrival, he reflected ironically. Lilian's whereabouts – as well as what dangerous situation she might be in – were impossible for him to know. He would have to take the chance of interrupting her, however busy she was.

At that precise moment, if he had known it, the object of his thoughts was standing outside the mayor's office at the Town Hall waiting to have the weekly meeting that she had insisted on fitting into both of their routines on taking over her post. It didn't overly excite him, but he had graciously conceded -for the benefit of the voters, naturally.

They discussed any problems that were taking place, talked over any foreseen obstacles to be overcome or, in the event of neither cases being relevant, just generally exchange ideas or proposals as to the smooth upkeep of the peace.

The Chief of Police looked at her watch impatiently; things were running with their habitual delay. As Roger poured a second cup of coffee, Lilian decided to do the same. The drinks machine was at the end of the corridor in sight of the mayor's office. If and when his secretary stepped out to advise her that he was ready, she wouldn't miss her.

As she stood sipping her piping hot beverage, a couple of civil servants approached with the hope of shrugging off the post weekend malaise. Amid sighs of gratitude for the needed tonic, they started commenting on the disagreeable task they had been set for the day. They had been charged with notifying the Parks Department of the orders they had received; orders concerning the immediate transfer of the animals at the zoo – once all of the necessary arrangements had been made concerning their health, safe carriage and the finding of their new living spaces. The last requirement was to be taken with laxity, as the priority was to get them out double quick; where, wasn't a matter of great concern.

Lilian threw the plastic cup into the container without finishing it and confronted the two weary faces, although she had no authority over them.

"Do you mean the gorillas are to go, as well?" she asked sternly.

"I don't know," one of them answered obediently, "anything that is in the zoo has to be out by the day after tomorrow at the latest. That's the council's decision."

The head of the police department strode towards the mayor's office, knocked once and went in without a gesture of courtesy. To her indignation, but not her surprise, she found him sitting in his leather chair, chatting and laughing away with his secretary. She jumped down spritely from the edge of the desk where she had been more than engrossed in the politicians more than likely absurd talk.

"Chief Ortega," said the politician in his overly pleasant voice, "do come in. Pamela – that's to say Miss Jones – was just finishing her rundown on my schedule for today. That will be all for now," he said, addressing the somewhat flustered employee, who picked up a folder that supposedly contained the supposed agenda and made her way towards the door – not before giving the ill-mannered intruder a scornful look as she closed it behind her.

"I see that you are a little peeved at the delay, but official business so often drags on, doesn´t it? You know that yourself. In any case, accept my apologies; I know you are a busy woman. Take a seat and let´s begin. What do we have for today´s meeting?"

"There is no ´today´s meeting´, she answered mocking his slimy tone. "I´ve just canceled it," she finished with a growl.

"Oh, have you indeed?" he said taken aback by her unexpected boldness. "Under what pretext? Has something important come up?"

"You bet it has." Lilian put both hands on the mayor´s oak-wood desk, leaned forward like a snake preparing to strike and, as blunt as a truncheon, said, "what the hell are you playing at with the permission for the gorilla park? Why have you turned it down after promising Mr. Penrose that it was all but signed and sealed?"

If Lilian´s opinion of politicians had before now bordered on the contemptuous, her opponent´s change of disposition from the worried ruler to the sly fox, obliged her to reconsider; it now became one of disgust, while the act of listening to his discourse was like trying not to throw up when your morning-after stomach is churning.

"So, it´s Mr. Penrose´s concern you have in mind, is it?" he said with a smirk that she would gladly have wiped clean, if she thought that it would have made a difference to the outcome. "Lilian, Lilian," he continued without delving into the matter any further – but knowing that he had struck a nerve that he thought would incline the argument in his favour, "you don´t seem to understand how things happen around here. I´m not a petit dictator who can impose his will on the other members of the council, however beneficial my intentions might be. The mayor has to bow to their rightful decision."

The police officer was now raging. "Bullshit. You solved the auction conveniently enough, the authority over the zoo was transferred without a hitch, and now you pretend to give me that ´democracy wins´ crap. You´re to blame and I want to know why you went back on your word. You were the one who talked him into buying the mansion, zoo animals included." She was now raging mad.

"If you are quite finished, I´m sure you have a job to do catching criminals, which is what you get paid for, and not for worrying about what happens to some dumb animals," he replied arrogantly. He added that he wasn´t about to be browbeaten by some jumped up detective who owed her status to him, adding insult to injury. His adversary wasn´t finished yet, though.

"I´ve given it a lot of thought," she said, "and I know why you kicked me upstairs. Let me tell you that you are not going to get away with this!"

The mayor changed his smirk for a defensive but defiant look. "Don't threaten me," he said, before returning to his sickeningly smug attitude. "Always assuming I know what you're hinting at. I assure you; I don't."

Seeing no further point in dealing with 'this slimy, shameless son of a bitch', Lilian turned her back on him, went to the exit and slammed the door closed, glad to be out of his obnoxious presence.

Her phone was in her hand and quickly connecting with her father's, but the answer was as expected; no, he didn't have Roger's number. It was a waste of time that she knew to be using as an excuse for not doing what she swore she would never do; return to the 'happy couple's home'. Now there was no choice but to face her demons, if she wanted to help the man who had shattered her dreams from having his own dreams broken by a buffoon like the one she had just left. Fortunately, she was courageous enough to overcome such mean feelings – all for the benefit of the gorillas, she told herself.

In an instant she was shooting out of the car park in her yellow vintage sports car, destination… the unknown. How would he – and she – react to her appearance, she asked herself while breaking all the existing speed limits. The automobile soon came roaring into the pebbled driveway, skillfully avoided an outgoing taxicab, came sliding to a stop at the front entrance, and the driver was out with an agility that only her well trained, adrenalin boosted body permitted.

Roger was there, open-mouthed, alongside Cynthia who had right at that moment been dropped off by the startled taxi driver. Lilian ran to the owner of the estate.

"The gorillas," she cried, breathing heavily with emotion. "they're to be taken away. You have to do something – now!"

The lord of the manor, overwhelmed with emotion at Lilian's arrival, was now sent reeling by what he had heard from her lips. Cynthia looked at him passively, apparently untouched by what was taking place before her eyes. Roger pulled himself together quicker than she had imagined; the meaning of what Lilian was saying worked its way into his interior, although he still made no sign of taking action.

"Roger, do you know what I'm saying?" the Chief of Police shouted again, "the mayor has ordered their transfer for tomorrow or the next day at the latest."

"Tomorrow?" he yelled, coming out of his catharsis once and for all. "Come on Cynthia, let's go have a talk with that traitor."

She hesitated just long enough for it to be plain to see that she wasn't particularly excited about the idea. In an attempt at covering her negative disposition, she answered, "but Lilian's convertible only has two seats. In any case, I have to freshen up. You go and I´ll hold the fort."

Roger wasn´t in the mood for discussions, so he ran to the vehicle with Lilian following right behind. She started the engine and drove off the in the same fashion with which she had entered – neither of them looked back.

They arrived at the Town Hall, jumped from the car and entered the seat of local democracy with the help of the Chief of Police´s identification – all in vain. The object of their search was already on his way out of town, they were politely informed. So, after Lilian left a message asking the fatuous absentee to get in contact with her as soon as he was able, they went back to the car with some disappointment and not a little anxiety. What if the scoundrel didn´t come back on time? Lilian took her place at the wheel, Roger on foot, musing beside her.

"What now?" the driver asked.

"I don´t know; we can only wait, I suppose," he said, still rummaging around in his mind. "Listen," he suddenly said, plucking up courage, "after what´s happened between us, why are you doing all of this for me?"

"Because you care for the animals; they´ve become your proposition in life. Isn´t that the most important thing? Isn´t that a fountain of inspiration for happiness? That is what you came here for, right? I know your opinion of me doesn't score high on the rankings, but do you think so little of me as to believe that I could just stand by and witness how someone else's happiness is taken away, stolen from them?"

"My god, you sound exactly like......" he said - or rather, he didn't say, unable to finish the sentence.

"Cynthia?", said Lilian with a wry smile.

The ex-broker looked into her eyes, awash with emotion. He decided there and then that it was high time to try out Jack's advice. "Listen," he said with firmness, "I have something important to look into. Thanks for your help, but this I have to do alone. I'll let you get on with your tasks."

A bit cold, admittedly, but it was the best he could do under the circumstances.

"Very well," she answered as evenly as she could. She wished him luck with his assignment and took off.

Roger watched her driving away, his heart on tenterhooks. What would be the outcome of his 'assignment'? he asked himself; what did he wish it to be? Just as when he had told her to leave him the day at the zoo when she had given herself so completely, he still tried to deny what he knew to be true. With a sigh, he hailed a taxicab, soon to find himself sitting at the very table where it had all begun. The thought surprised him; "where it had all begun" he said again, as if the repeated chanting of the phrase would reveal some sense hidden within it. He was interrupted by the owner of the ice-cream parlor asking for his order.

"I'm waiting for someone to join me, we'll order when she arrives," he said. "On second thoughts, bring me a coffee meanwhile, please."

A sip was taken from the cup while he carefully marked, first one and then the other, the numbers of the two woman who had taken a place in his life ever since his arrival in what seemed like an age ago. The messages were duly sent; now he had only to await who Jack had termed 'the girl for him'. It was a quaint little choice of words, maybe too much so in a world where such usage was frowned upon as old fashioned – another of his friend's relics from another time.

He turned the phone off, so as not to receive the message he was sure would come from one of the two; he wanted the surprise to take place there in the ice-cream parlour – in the flesh, so to speak.

The street in which it was situated had nothing much to offer by way of interest for the eyes, so he closed them and went back to being the kid full of excitement at the thought of having his first 'date'. Then he was re-living the embarrassment of how it finished, although, now that he thought about it, he realized that it was nothing more than a funny prank, the kind that all nervous adolescents play on each other all the time.

So engrossed was he in his reminiscing that he was unaware of the smile plastered all over his face. Neither was he conscious of the tinkling of the small bell which hung above the door, signaling the entrance of a new client. When he lifted the lids that had shut out reality for those few wonderfully unreal moments, he saw that there were two chocolate sundaes on the table; one for him, one for the woman who had bought them -and who was now sitting opposite.

"You remembered the flavor," he said, his voice quivering with emotion.

"How could I forget? This time I´ll let you eat it while you tell me what´s so important."

Roger was at a loss as to what to say, except for telling her the real reason behind the summons. Before he could, however, her phone rang and the mayor was promptly telling her of his return and that he would be available in his office for the rest of the day, if she wanted to see her.

"Come on," Lilian said after hanging up, "I´m afraid you can´t eat your ice-cream today, either; the Mayor is waiting in his office."

"No, I have a better idea," he replied. "Tell him you have to meet him at the Mansion."

"The Mansion? Why?" Lilian asked with trepidation; she'd been there once today already and she wasn't sure if she could handle another visit.

"Just tell him, that's all. I have questions that need answers; and I believe I'll find them there."

"Alright. If that's what you want, I'll try and persuade him to meet you at your home. Good luck with the answers."

"No, no. You are coming too. I need you... to unravel the enigma that will lead to the saving of my gorillas. I think *you* have the solution. Will you come?"

The head of the police department could see what Roger was getting at when he talked about her knowing something that would force a solution and had already guessed what the plan involved. With a look of tacit agreement between them, they left for the showdown.

For the first time since his arrival at the sea-side town, his mind was clear and his heart was pounding with joy, but right then wasn't the moment to let the woman beside him know his feelings.

Chapter Fifteen

When they drove through the estate grounds up to the house, they saw the mayor's car parked right at the foot of the steps which led to the main entrance. He was standing at the door talking to Cynthia, both of them asking what this was all about. Roger and Lilian walked up the steps towards them with the explanation they had quickly agreed on while making the short journey.

"Mr. Penrose," said the politician seriously, completely ignoring his Chief of Police, "I imagine you want to talk about the council's decision to refuse a license for your project. But that could have been handled perfectly well at the Town Hall, don't you think? In any case, as I told your companion this very morning, it's completely out of my hands. In fact, I'm just as disappointed as you are."

"You're lying, Roland; you know it, I know it and detective Ortega knows it too," said Roger with self-assurance.

"My dear fellow," retorted the mayor with what was supposed to be indignation, but it didn't fool anyone present.

"My dear fellow," mocked Lilian, "as *I* said this morning, I'm in a position, thanks to you, to oblige you to get the council to turn round on their decision -and then hand in your resignation."

"And that's exactly what you are going to do this afternoon," added the estate owner. "So, get onto your colleagues, arrange an extraordinary sitting, and I'll call by to pick up the papers first thing tomorrow."

"Well, well, you are in league with one another, is that it? Let me tell you; there's nothing you can do or say that will make me change the way things are. Therefore, if you don't mind, I'll take my leave – I've already wasted enough time coming here. Good day Cynthia."

"Aren't you at least curious about why you were invited to our little get-together?" Lilian said to the receding figure, "you haven't heard what Cynthia has to say."

Her statement took everyone by surprise, especially the expensively dressed town ruler, who stopped and turned. He was more than curious; he was frightened.

"You see," continued Lilian," she's going to order you, her good friend, to do exactly what Mr. Penrose and I have told you to do. If not, I'll re-open the case of your predecessor's premature demise. I've already done some unofficial investigations, and it would seem that her DNA is on the flower he was holding in his hand so tightly that she couldn't get it from him. Something that was somehow 'overlooked' by the officers who took over the case."

Cynthia laughed scornfully, while her answer gave Roger the impression that she had regained the composure that he was used to seeing. One of the first leaves of the approaching autumn came to rest on her shoulder. She took it between her elegant hands and crushed it, a graphic way of emphasizing her verdict on Lilian's accusations.

"Why naturally," she said as she let fall the crumpled leaf, "you gave it to me to examine, remember? Listen, dear, you'll have to come up with something a little more convincing for the jury."

"A pertinent observation, *my lady*," Lilian replied, showing a confidence that the mayor took for downright insolence towards a member of the aristocracy. She ignored him completely, concentrating on Cynthia. "The only trouble is…"

Lilian paused, deliberately tensing the chord, as well as attempting to do the same with her two opponent's nerves: making the drama interminable. As for the Mayor, who had to make use of a silk hanky to wipe away the sweat from his forehead, it was becoming unbearable. At last, the detective continued.

"… the only mistake you are making is that the flower you examined was one I picked from a greenhouse, not the one in the victim's hand."

The one-time philosopher looked at the mayor for some support. When none came, she again faced the Chief of Police, incredulous. Seeing her foe's resistance wavering, Lilian gladly let fall what she believed would be the definitive punch.

"If you are found guilty, you surely won't let your accomplice go free to reap the rewards of the crime you both planned. Are you going to let him off the hook while you spend the rest of your days and nights looking at the world from behind bars? I do hear it's most frustrating, especially for someone like you, used to being immersed in nature."

"Now just a god damned minute," the alluded to politician tried to say, before being cut short by the Lady Waverley.

"Don't bother Roland; she obviously has a case against us," she said sharply, and then turned back to Lilian, slowing the tempo of her words. "I assume you also found *his* strands of double helix all over the plant."

"Of course."

What appeared to be the final act of the spectacle turned out to be no more than an interlude when Cynthia suddenly straightened up both her stance, as well as her strength of will. In spite of her own growing repulsion towards the politician, she glimpsed a solution.

"Stop trembling like the coward you are, Roland," she said, coolly addressing the mayor. "I wouldn't worry about going to jail, if I were you."

"No?"

"Not at all. You see, Detective Ortega, despite everything, won´t formally accuse you; in fact, she is going to leave things exactly as they are. Am I not right, Lilian?"

"Is that right?" the officer asked, fascinated by what she had just heard. She was beginning to suspect some hidden intentions behind the statement but, fearless, she continued with the dialectic battle between the two unshakeable women. "And just why would I do such a thing?"

"Quite simple: if you press charges against him, he´ll be obliged to confess to fixing Roger´s auction bid, since it really took place. If that comes about, the new owner will no longer be so. He´ll lose the estate and all that goes with it – gorillas included. Wouldn´t that defeat your purpose, as well as being a terrible shame?"

Cynthia had now completely recovered her calm disposition, even allowing herself the pleasure of a subtle, but complacent smile. Roger saw that it was his turn to step in with the answer.

"Consider this, then, Cynthia; if I lose the estate, it will be sold to the highest bidder. I personally know of a few investors who would have no qualms about turning the grounds into a Hotel Complex, or maybe an Adventure Park. I´ve also heard about a very rich business-man who is very interested in building a very upper-crust casino in this neck of the woods."

Cynthia hadn't considered that eventuality, and it showed. Roger recognized, not without a little sadness, that she was losing the fragile serenity conquered beforehand. Nonetheless, he brought his mind back to focusing on the task at hand. The game they were playing had reached a stalemate; one of the sides would have to yield their position. He made a surprising decision.

"Cynthia, why don't you and I have a chat together? Inside, alone."

"Hold on a second," she said, standing firm as the estate owner took her arm. "I'm curious about something – or someone, I should say." She fixed her gaze once again on the Chief of Police. "Are you willing to let things be, if I persuade the mayor to settle things in Roger's favor? What about your oath to bring criminals to justice."

The policewoman didn't hesitate in her reply, "As far as I can see, handcuffing you two would only mean an uncertain – possibly even unpleasant – future for the gorillas, the estate, not to mention the town in general."

Their eyes locked as if they were attempting to read each other's thoughts. In the end, Cynthia shrugged her shoulders and said simply, "That sounds reasonable enough. Besides, the victim was a vile caricature of a human being." She then turned and accompanied Roger inside.

They stood in the hall, visible to the other two outside, in conversation for a good while. Lilian began to show signs of nervousness, becoming unbearable as the two inside drew closer to one another. The she saw how Roger took Cynthia´s hands then fused in an emotional embrace.

When the two disentwined, the politician ran in seeking the Lady´s verdict, while Roger sauntered out in search of Lilian. They were both disappointed; Cynthia ´proposed´ the mayor should settle the issue of the building permit and hurriedly resign just as he had been told to do, while Lilian had made an even quicker getaway.

Roger stood where the two had stood during the interaction with the two who were now inside, looked back towards the door and understood why she had decided to go without a word; he could see Cynthia and Roland in conversation through the glass, just as Lilian would have seen his with Her Ladyship – embrace included. Oddly enough, he felt strangely serene about it all. He whistled a familiar tune from his younger days as he made his way round the side of the house to where his Spider was parked.

On his way into town, he had to stop at a traffic light in red – and there was Jack, waiting to cross the road. As he did, he saw who the driver was and greeted his friend warmly. "Roger, how are things going?"

"Never better," he replied.

"Did our little plan work at all? Did you discover the identity of the little urchin with the ice-cream?"

"You bet," Roger ended with a smile that had happiness written all over it. He drove on, only to hear his friend get the habitual last word, "I knew who it was all along..."

Only two or three minutes separated him from his destination, so that the bell above the ice-cream parlour door was soon sounding its pleasant-to-the-ear tinkling. The place was empty, except for one solitary client sitting eating a chocolate sundae. Roger took a seat calmly opposite the surprised figure who, in her surprise, was almost unable to hold back the rising ocean currents of emotion that welled up from the depths once again.

"I thought I would find you here," the contented newcomer said with a look that said that he was also more than glad that she was. His relaxed demeanor proved to be his downfall: in a movement as agile as any teenager might be capable of, the young lady had run out without a word, leaving behind a young man with a tub of ice-cream encrusted in his joyous face. He had to laugh, of course, as he took a paper napkin and wiped it clean.

"I think this time you should go after her," shouted the owner, laughing along with Roger.

"I think you're right," he answered, taking for granted that things would naturally unfold exactly as he had imagined they would on his way here. "See you around," he added as he got to the door where he took a right turn, heading down to the street around whose corner he knew to be parked the now famous yellow sports car. Lilian was sitting in the passenger seat, so Roger opened the driver's door and took his place at the steering wheel.

"I felt sure you would come," she said, mirroring Roger's earlier greeting, although the same couldn't be said about the tone in which it was delivered. "I'm puzzled as to why, however."

"I don't blame you, after what you saw back at the house," Roger answered, either ignoring or not perceiving Lilian's disposition. He explained with perfect sincerity the conversation in which Cynthia had agreed to go along with his 'proposition', finally saying their last goodbyes with a hug.

"You appear to be very skilled at that, I see," said the attractive officer with an expression on her face that reminded Roger perilously of that of their first meeting. "At saying goodbye, I mean," she finished with what sounded like a prelude to doom.

The stupid look on his face told Lilian that the financial whiz kid, now turned naturalist, had begun to feel the first inkling of his immense error of judgment. Indeed, the roles had changed since she had confided her heart to this fool of a man who now pretended to act as if things could be mended by ignoring their never having happened. She started the engine up and the suspicion became self-evident.

"Roger," she said trying not to sound disdainful, much less cruel. "Do you seriously think that you can turn up, magnanimously accept what you had the chance of having in the Spring after having trodden it underfoot and then spent the summer with another woman? I don´t know how your ´quest´ is coming along, but in my opinion you´re far from succeeding. In other words - and I hope you´re taking note of how well I´m dealing with all of this – I hope you´ll find happiness alone there in your stately home. Goodbye."

Lilian looked in the rearview mirror at Roger who was recovering from the gently dispensed shock and valiantly recognizing the truth in every word. She decided that she hadn´t quite finished, hit the break and skillfully backed up to the spot where the reflective ´fool´ was still rooted. She got out of the car and swayed towards him.

"It just occurred to me that I might be wrong in my assessment," she said calmly, giving wing to Roger´s sudden hopes of reconciliation. "Your attitude is so clearly child-like that perhaps you have achieved your goal. Just a thought. Good-day."

The astute woman's ironic words and the well-played parody of her father's closing intervention on the opening night, pleased her greatly. She graciously refused to show it openly, simply turning on her heels, getting back in the car and driving off once again before allowing a sweet smile to smile bitterly back at her in the mirror. The same mirror in which she watched Roger receding from her view; from her life; but not from her memory.

Once the vintage car had been lost in the distance he had nothing to do but search out his own, hindered by the gloom that surrounded him. He found it almost by chance and was quickly on the road with the westering sun behind him and what was his now deserted residence ahead; which naturally made him recall the phrase said to the estate agent when he so lightheartedly left the keys of his house with him; which of course made him ask if it had been a premonition, or a self-fulfilling prophecy, or both, or neither. The only thing he did feel certain about was that he certainly was in a muddle.

Chapter Sixteen

Without Roger being aware of it and just as he was parking his car, Lilian, despite her earlier assuredness, was driving out of town feeling the same confusion, while Cynthia was sadly closing the door to her little shed come bed-sit, suitcase in hand.

A short while later the forecasted rain began to fall on the gardener's covered head as she sat waiting for the bus into town; Lilian had stopped and was hurriedly raising the car roof, while Roger was stood looking out over the beautiful park that was his and his alone. He loved the way the rain slanted slightly, pushed by the breeze that the two women were finding so bothersome.

Suddenly he was the youngster again, his timeless gaze looking back over the fields and the canal that he and his friends had just intrepidly crossed in search of bird nests and the eggs hopefully contained therein. Concretely, those of the ducks or quails who inhabited the area that suited exactly their needs. Two of them had taken flight right then, probably frightened by the presence of the youngsters, or as a ruse to lead them away from the nests hidden amongst the knee-high grass.

He then turned away from both the park and the memory to what would now be his only passion, namely the gentle giants who were all now as sheltered as they could be from the weather. Yes, he said to himself as droplets of sweet water fell from his nose, enough of living in the past: tomorrow the landscapers would set to work on his project, the one that depended on no one but himself.

Cynthia paid her fare and took her seat on an appropriately empty bus, thinking of the future that awaited her. Going back to the academic world was always a possibility, but she felt an uncomfortable twinge in her stomach at the thought. She had been invited to stay on as groundkeeper at the park, even to help out with the animals, although the prospect of having to work on what was once her estate and alongside the new owners, as she imagined would be the case, wasn't exactly one that thrilled her to bits. No, she had no choice except to leave the past behind and disappear into the unknown.

Lilian was also on her way towards her own destination, with one difference: hers was well known beforehand, now that she had already asked for a transfer to another town. She was, however, sitting on the car bonnet with her thoughts, not caring for the rain that was leaving her drenched. She knew she had one last thing to do before abandoning the town, something necessary if she wanted to resolve the conflicts of the past and it consisted of a visit to the woman who had been the object of her resentment since she was a young and innocent girl -and the price would be a lofty one, she knew. It had to be done, nonetheless: if not, she would always be encumbered with the need to return sometime sooner or later, and she didn't want that, did she? Lilian then decided to get back into her car, leaving that last question aside, unanswered.

"Silently falls the rain, eh?" said a familiar, and more than welcome voice at Roger's side. "You seem to have a predilection for the rainy season."

"Jack," responded the drenched and solitary young man with delight. "Funnily enough, it has been recently said that I'm still wet behind the ears."

The policeman laughed along with his friend; his daughter had put him in the picture as to today's events. He duly did the same, telling Roger of Lilian's decision to look for new horizons – and why!

"So, it looks as if we're alone here you and I, doesn't it?"

Roger agreed with melancholic resignation before realizing the consequences for the proud father who had so thoughtfully come to comfort *him*.

"It must be hard for you. I'm sorry, it is in great part my fault," he said with sorrow.

"Oh, don't punish yourself so, Roger. It's only a natural step in any father's life. You'll miss her too, if I'm not mistaken."

The alluded to didn't answer there and then, rather he turned the conversation to the other half of the duo who had occupied his recent life. "Tell me your opinion on Cynthia. Disappointing, wouldn't you say? I never suspected that she could be involved in such a crime."

"But she wasn't involved directly, according to my Lil. Didn't she tell you? The idea was to use the phony DNA thing to trap the mayor into more or less admitting that he had had a hand in it, and so get him to unblock the transfer of the gorillas. With Cynthia's help, of course. You see, she caught on quickly and, thankfully, decided to play along with Lilian's story. Her only offence was to use what she had found out to get the politician to stop your project."

"With the aim of saving her ancestral home. Understandable, I suppose," said Roger with a sigh. "So, being innocent and, therefore, aware of your daughter's bluff, why did she finally collaborate with Lilian and allow my project to go ahead?"

"Perhaps because it was *your* project," was the only thing the officer could think of as way of an answer. "Hey," he went on after a moments silence, "whatever happened to that postcard of yours? Did you resolve the enigma, or will it remain a mystery?"

The landowner looked at the sly old fox and sniggered good naturedly. "If you have spoken to your beloved offspring, then you already know the answer, Sergeant. Or at least, her inestimable opinion on the subject. As for me, I don't really know what to say. I've certainly had the most exhilarating summer ever, surpassing those of my childhood. On the other hand, I'm left once again with only memories."

"And the scars," Jack added in his usual down to earth way of speaking. "Don't give up hope, though: you've learned a lot about yourself, I'm sure. All part of growing older."

"And wiser?" asked Roger with gentle irony.

"Well, that's a question and a half," Jack laughed, drawing the attention of the great silver-back who was slowly chewing on a shrub, impervious of the philosophical considerations of the two drenched figures on the other side of the fence. "I like to think so, although I wouldn't presume to be anything other than plain old me."

"Well then, plain old you," Roger laughed in his turn, apparently having shrugged off the last vestiges of gloom," the only thing I know is this: I'm young; the owner of a piece of aristocratic history together with its beautiful surroundings; for the first time I have a soul-stirring goal in life; and I've just lived the most exhilarating summer of my life."

"Do you know, Roger, I have Lilian's new address. I know a nice little pub in town where, if you invite me for a pint, I could let you have it. You could always right another post-card."

"Yes, but who would I send it to?"